HOLD ME
UNTIL MORNING

a Grayson Brothers novel

CHRISTINA
PHILLIPS

Entangled Publishing, LLC
2614 South Timberline Road
Suite 109
Fort Collins, CO 80525
Visit our website at www.entangledpublishing.com.

Brazen is an imprint of Entangled Publishing, LLC. For more information on our titles, visit www.brazenbooks.com.

Edited by Candace Havens
Cover design by Heather Howland
Cover art from Hot Damn Stock

Manufactured in the United States of America

First Edition September 2015

ENTANGLED
BRAZEN

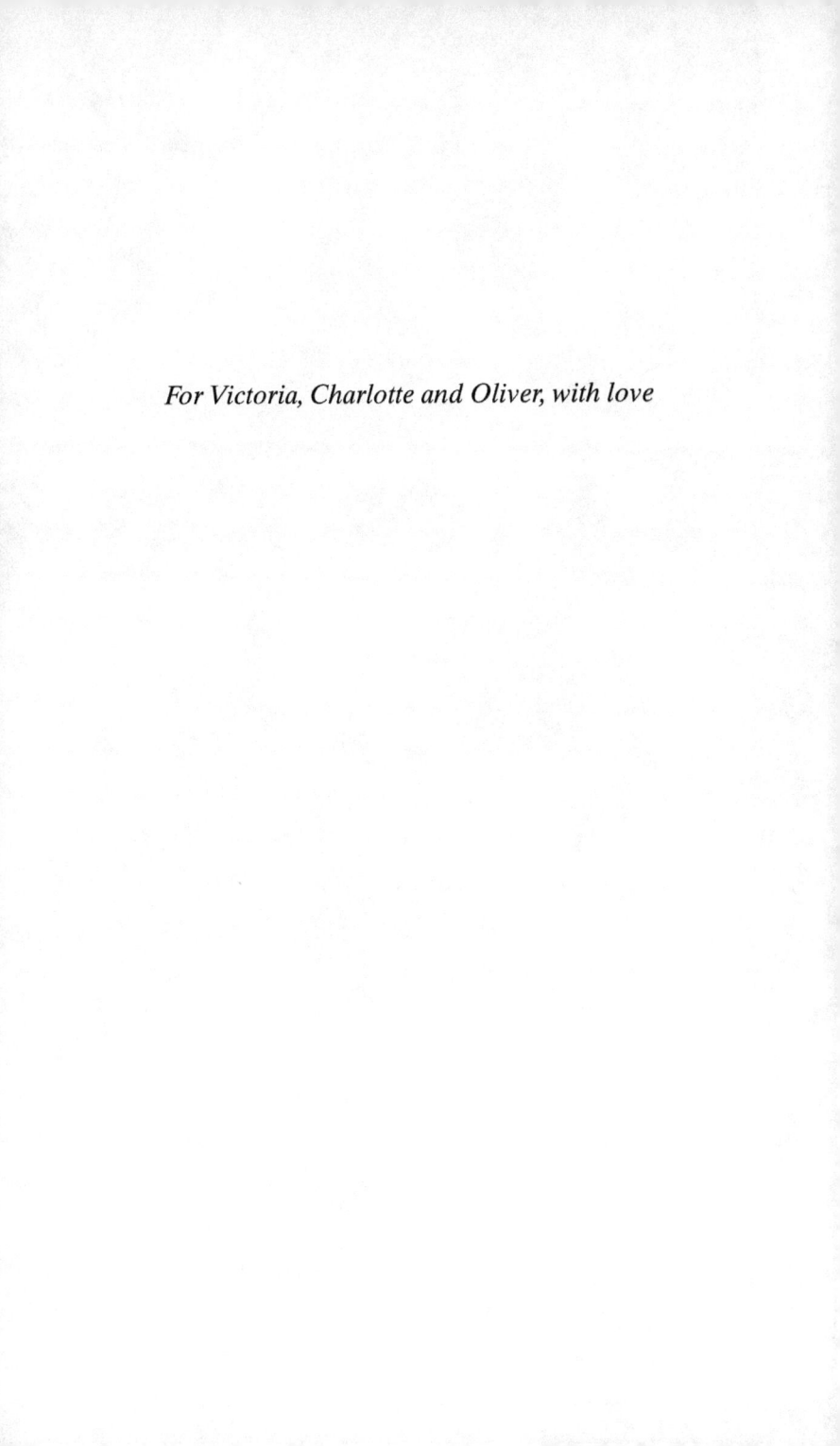

For Victoria, Charlotte and Oliver, with love

Chapter One

Cooper Grayson killed the engine of his Harley Sportster and eyed the run down mountain cabin set back from the dirt track that passed as a road. When his best friend Scott had given him directions to this hideaway in the San Gabriel Mountains, he'd forgotten to mention it was in need of total renovation.

He swung his leg over the bike, hung his helmet over the handlebar, and walked toward the one-story building, his boots crunching on the gravel. Every step he took reinforced his conviction that he'd been a damn fool to agree to Scott's request.

How the hell was he going to keep a high maintenance Hollywood soap star safe in this shithole? Sure, the place was isolated enough to keep all but the most obsessed fans or paparazzi from finding it. He didn't mind the wilderness or very basic facilities, but he wasn't thinking about himself here.

Paris Annabelle Sofia O'Connell loved the good things in life — top hotels, four-star restaurants, and shopping sprees that could allegedly fund a small country.

No way she'll be happy here.

But of course, he'd said yes when Scott had asked the favor three days ago. She was Scott's little sister, and Cooper and Paris had practically grown up together.

Who else could Scott trust to not only make sure Paris was safe but also keep his mouth shut?

Cooper squinted through the window by the side of the front door. His faint hope that the entire place was renovated, and equipped with all the luxuries Paris was now used to, vanished. From what he could see of the kitchen, it looked as though it hadn't been touched for about seventy years.

Something snagged his attention. New window bolts had been fitted to the old frames. He stepped back. Obviously Scott had sorted out some kind of security when Paris had decided to "disappear" for a while.

He glanced around at the willows that draped into the stream not far from the property, then at the forest backdrop on one side and the canyon to the east. Whatever else Paris's newly acquired hideaway lacked, a kick-ass view wasn't it.

The sound of an engine throbbed in the distance. Cooper strolled back to his bike and watched the dust rise on the dirt road as Scott's SUV raced toward the cabin. Cooper hadn't seen Paris for ten years, not since the day her mom had swept her off to the dizzying heights of a starring role in some trashy prime time soap.

But he'd certainly seen her on the TV and magazine covers. It was hard to miss her when she was the darling of Hollywood and the face of an exclusive cosmetics company.

He shifted his weight from one foot to the other and let out a sigh. Babysitting spoiled rich girls wasn't something he'd done before. He might have once thought of Paris as his little sister, but those days had long since gone. It didn't matter what Scott said about her being the same girl she'd always been. He knew he couldn't be that lucky.

The car skidded to a stop, inches from his bike, spraying up dust and gravel. He glared into the tinted windows. Who was Scott trying to impress? It was only his sister in the car.

The driver's door swung open and a slender figure emerged, wearing a Giants baseball cap jammed onto shoulder-length black hair, and a faded Giants sweatshirt. It sure as hell wasn't Scott. It didn't look anything like Paris, either, as she strolled toward the back of the car.

Still frowning, he made his way around the front of the SUV. The driver, hands on hips, appeared to be focused on a distant mountain peak, and ignored his approach.

There was no one else in the car. He raked his gaze over the back of the silent figure. She might not resemble the girl from his childhood, but she had to be Paris.

He pushed the car door shut. Her gorgeous tanned legs came into view, along with sexy denim shorts that barely covered her cute ass.

Whoa. Whatever else he did this week, he definitely wasn't hitting on his best friend's little sister.

So stop looking at her ass.

"Paris?"

She slowly turned around. Massive sunglasses hid her eyes, but there was no mistaking those pouty lips, or the face that had been described as angelic by those who hadn't known her as a daredevil kid.

"Hey, Cooper." Her voice was husky, as though she'd just woken up, and graphic images flashed through his mind, of her tangled in bed sheets wearing nothing but her own designer perfume.

Damn. She's hot. Guilt prickled down his spine. Scott'd rip his head off if he knew the dirty thoughts running through Cooper's mind right now.

It's going to be a long week.

Not for the first time, Paris was relieved she could hide behind the dark shades she wore every time she left the house. Usually it was so she never made accidental eye contact with the paparazzi that tailed her like a bad smell. Right now it had more to do with the fact that she couldn't tear her fascinated gaze from the vision that was Cooper Grayson.

She'd been mad as hell when Scott had told her he'd hired his old childhood friend as her bodyguard for this week. She didn't care that he'd trust Cooper with his life, or that Cooper was in the private security business.

This week was her last chance to get away from everything and clear her head before she confronted her mom about her future. No one knew about this hideaway, and the chances of the paparazzi finding her were low, considering she'd left a false trail to Europe. She'd only caved when her brother had told her if she didn't say yes to Cooper, then Scott would come with her instead.

No matter how much he loved his firefighting job, she knew her brother better than to think he was bluffing about taking time off work. So she'd agreed, and then taken his car as payback.

But one look at Cooper managed to suck every resentful thought from her head. And that was before he said her name in that sexy rumble.

He was nothing like the faded memories of the devil-may-care fourteen-year-old boy from when they'd lived in the same rundown neighborhood.

She was having a hard time tearing her gaze from his breathtaking biceps, which bulged just the right amount. *How would it feel to have those arms around me?* She licked her lips and tried to shove the thought from her mind.

Except she couldn't get past the way his black T-shirt stretched over his impressive chest.

Holy crap. His pecs are to die for.

All the bodyguards she'd had over the last few years had been built—it was a requirement of the job—but not one of them had caused a single lustful thought to surface. She hadn't been in Cooper's company for two minutes, and all she could think about was getting naked with him.

Never going to happen.

That didn't stop her face heating.

God, she hoped he thought she was suffering from sun-stroke or something. It was one thing for strangers to think she had the same trashy morals as Lola, her *Sunset Heights* character, but for some reason she didn't want him thinking it.

They hadn't seen each other for ten years, and they were as good as strangers. He probably didn't even remember her from when she lived across the street from him. Unlike some from her past, when she'd made it big he hadn't crawled out of the woodwork to share tales of her childhood with the tabloids.

"Need a hand with your gear?"

His question, so totally down to earth and non-sexual, managed to shatter her paralysis, and she finally dragged her attention to his face. Stubble grazed his strong jaw, and his eyes were hidden behind a pair of shades, but it was the dimple in his right cheek that mesmerized her.

His slow grin sent a familiar shock through her. As a kid, she'd always had a crush on him. Even though her mom thought he was the *wrong* kind of boy. Jesus, they hadn't known what the *wrong* kind of boy was until they arrived in Hollywood.

Still, he had that sense of danger about him.

She cleared her throat, but it did nothing to clear the haze of lust that fogged her brain. "Sure." She hoped he didn't notice how hoarse she sounded. "In the trunk."

When he strolled to the back of the car, she took a deep breath and pulled her purse and carryall from the front seat. Instead of spending a relaxing week getting her shit together, she was now going to have to battle the urge to jump her bodyguard's bones.

Why couldn't he have as much sex appeal as her other ones? In other words, *none*. Her last bodyguard had made her want to barf.

She slammed the car door to cut off that line of thought. "Fuck me."

Paris followed Cooper to see what the problem was. He was staring into the trunk as though he couldn't believe his eyes.

"I thought we were only staying here a week?"

"That's right. Scott always nags that I pack way too much." *Is that what you think as well?*

Cooper made a sound in the back of his throat. She wasn't sure whether it was a snort or a strangled laugh. "Scott's a dick."

Paris blinked. She wasn't used to people telling her that her brother was a dick. It wasn't the kind of thing anyone would say if they were trying to get on her good side.

He obviously didn't care about keeping on her good side. On the other hand, Scott *could* be a dick, and who would know that better than his oldest friend?

"I think he's proud of that fact." It drove their mom mad that Scott refused to kiss ass for the furtherance of Paris's career. At twelve, she hadn't seen what all the fuss was about. At sixteen, the tension between her brother and mother, on top of the expanding demands of her career, had stressed her out so much she'd ended up in rehab. The press reported it was because of an emotional breakdown. Only her immediate family and her agent knew it was because she'd developed an unhealthy obsession with *Absolut*.

"Scott's never changed." Cooper hauled out one of her bulging cases as though it weighed no more than a sack of feathers. *Phew.* Impressive. "I thought he was coming with you. You drove all the way from Hollywood on your own?"

It was hardly an epic journey. Before she could get too riled that he thought her incapable of driving herself anywhere, he lifted a second case from the trunk and shot her a smile that liquefied her insides like warm honey.

To distract herself from his sexy mouth and the obvious ease with which he handled her luggage, she slung her carryall over one shoulder and picked up her beauty case from the trunk.

"He was coming with me. I don't know why he thought that was a good idea. How did he expect me to get to the nearest town without a car once he left?"

He paused by the front door while she rummaged for the key in her purse.

"I have a bike. We wouldn't have been stranded."

She almost dropped the key at the thought of clinging to him as they raced along the mountainous roads. Now *that* would be an epic journey, for sure.

"I'm perfectly able to get some shopping by myself, without a bodyguard tailing me." She jammed the key into the new lock, but couldn't help shooting him a quick glance to see how he'd taken her remark, which had basically put him in his place. Not that he had given any indication that he was here for any other reason but to protect her. That was all in her tragically perverted mind.

She had to remember he was just her bodyguard for the week…and Scott's best friend. Two excellent reasons why she had to stop imagining how it would feel if she kissed him.

She kicked open the door and stepped inside. The sooner she got rid of her wig the better. It was obviously causing her brain to overheat.

"I won't tail you." He followed her into the cabin. The front room, which had seemed so cozy and adorable when she'd first looked at the property, now felt oddly cramped. "We can pretend we're a couple and hold hands. You're an actor, right? Shouldn't be too hard to pull that off."

She stared at him, momentarily speechless. Was he joking? Now that she thought about it, he had never taken anything seriously.

She pulled her floundering thoughts together and offered him one of Lola's sardonic smiles. She might've grown to loathe her soap opera character over the last year or so, but there was no doubt she sometimes came in handy.

"I might be able to pull that off, but what about you? Acting isn't always as easy as it looks."

"Yeah, it's going to kill me having to hold your hand and pretend I think you're gorgeous."

She was used to guys telling her she was gorgeous, beautiful, and sexy. There had been a time when she'd been flattered by all the attention, but that was before people she'd thought she could trust had totally screwed her over. For the last couple of years, all her cynical mind could think was *what do you want from me, buddy?*

Somehow her mind couldn't quite come up with the same suspicious response when it came to Cooper.

And then something occurred to her. He hadn't complimented her at all. He'd *actually* said he'd have to pretend to think she was gorgeous.

That was such a revelation that she let out a snort of laughter. Her mom would've died if she'd heard that sound. Cooper, on the other hand, just grinned. God, his dimple was cute, so much at odds with his tough, muscle-bound body. She had the alarming urge to stroke her finger over his cheek.

Get a grip. She couldn't spend the whole week thinking how hot Cooper Grayson was. What the hell had they been talking about anyway?

"I guess you can come with me when I take the car to get provisions." If she was going to compromise, then so was he. She waited to see what he made of that.

"Not keen to ride my Harley, huh?"

Riding his Harley was tempting. Riding *him* even more so.

"We can take turns. How's that?" Had she just committed herself to riding his bike? Was she mad? It'd been so long since she'd had sex, she'd probably rub herself up against his butt like a cat in heat. The vision was both horrifying and hideously alluring. Thank God he was still wearing his shades. Coupled with the subdued lighting inside, it made it unlikely he'd notice her mortified blush.

Best not to tempt fate, though. She turned and marched into the small hallway that led to the single bathroom and two bedrooms, both of which boasted fabulous views of the distant canyon.

"This is mine." She pushed open the door of the biggest room. Although *big* was only relative to the size of the place. The closet of her bedroom back in Beverly Hills was roomier.

He strolled in and dropped her luggage onto the bare timber floor. Then he pushed his shades onto his head and turned to face her. "Did you buy this place fully furnished?"

She dragged her sexually deprived mind away from admiring his gorgeous, deep brown eyes. If she got so turned on just by looking at his face, she hoped to God she never caught sight of him coming out of the shower wrapped only in a towel.

Liar. Now the image was burned for all time into the secret corners of her imagination.

With fake nonchalance she placed her carryall and case on the end of the antiqued brass framed double bed and pulled off her sunglasses. "No. I bought a few things at a couple of auctions last month and had them delivered here. This is kind of like my secret project."

So secret, even her mom didn't know about it.

At least she'd bought two beds in that last lot she bid on. Somehow she couldn't see Cooper getting comfortable for the night on the charming, overstuffed loveseat she'd acquired for the front room.

He strolled to the French doors, leaned one hand against the doorframe, and surveyed the view. Paris checked out his delectably tight butt encased in faded denim.

This week was going to kill her.

Cooper stared through the glass, but it wasn't the over-grown back yard or the hazy, blue-tinged mountains in the distance that captured his attention. Because his attention was all tangled up by the gorgeous green of Paris's eyes when she'd pulled off her shades.

Fuck, he needed to get out of this room. All he could think about was that bed. And Paris.

Concentrate. What were they talking about? "You went basic for a weekend retreat."

"Not really a five-star hotel, huh?"

He watched her ghostlike reflection in the glass as she opened the designer carryall she'd dropped onto the bed. *Get back to business.*

"Scott wasn't clear about the extent of my duties. Do they include bringing you breakfast in bed each morning?"

Why doesn't my big mouth ever listen to my brain?

"Yes, I definitely expect breakfast in bed each morning.

And don't forget the freshly squeezed orange juice."

He swung round to face her. "You bring a juicer with you?"

For a moment she stared at him. It was obvious she had absolutely no idea whether he was pulling her chain or serious, and while he'd been kidding about the whole breakfast thing, he was starting to change his mind.

"No, but there might be one in the kitchen. I had a box of stuff delivered a couple of days ago."

That must have been when Scott had called him and said Paris was exhausted and needed a break. According to the online gossip, she'd collapsed on set. Until now, it hadn't occurred to him to question it.

But if that *was* the real reason, wouldn't she be better off in some luxury retreat where she wouldn't have to lift a finger? Something didn't add up.

"So what's with—" The words died in his throat as she pulled off her hair.

She tossed the black wig onto the bed and shook her head, and her familiar red-gold curls tumbled over her shoulders. She plunged her fingers through her hair and gave it a good ruffle.

He stared at her, transfixed. She looked as though she'd just been thoroughly fucked.

Why the hell had he offered to bring her breakfast in bed? He was asking for trouble. Why couldn't she have been the spoiled brat he'd been expecting?

She let out a blissful sigh that didn't help the state of his erection at all, and looked at him. "What? Did you think that was my real hair?"

He hadn't thought about it at all, except to think it didn't look anything like her. "Guess it works," he conceded. "But I prefer your natural look."

"Flatterer." There was a mocking note in her voice, but she didn't look pissed off by his remark. "Just so you know, I'm immune to all that crap. It won't get you anywhere."

"Babe, I'm wounded you think I'm just trying to flatter you." He slammed his fist against his heart in the hope of detracting attention from his unruly cock. Not that she appeared the least bit interested in checking him out there. "I'm telling you the truth. No strings—or crap—attached."

She laughed. "That's a change. Okay then. Thank you." She gave an elaborate curtsey. "*Babe.*"

"You don't like me calling you *babe*?" He seriously needed to get out of this room while he was still capable of walking straight, but the smile on her face and the flirty glitter in her eyes were just too damn irresistible. "How about honeybee? Or sweetie-pie? Got to call you something when we're out in public."

"How about I call you my cuddly bunny?"

"I'm not the one going undercover."

She sighed. "Fine. *Babe* it is, but the point is to not draw any attention our way in the first place. So the less we actually say in public the better."

It wasn't worth telling her she would turn heads no matter what disguise she tried to hide behind. There was just something about her that made you take a second look.

"I won't let you say a word. You can count on me."

Instead of her laughing again, a strange, pensive expression crossed her face, and then she raked her gaze over his body, and lingered on his crotch.

Heat seared through him. Fuck, he was *not* blushing. No

girl had made him blush in living memory, and he definitely wasn't starting now. He strolled with pained indifference toward the door but had an absolute certainty that Paris's gaze never wavered from his butt.

A long week? It was going to be a long fucking *day*.

Chapter Two

A persistent knocking penetrated Paris's sleep-bound mind, and she squinted at her cell. What the hell? It was only seven in the morning. She rolled onto her back and pulled the sheet over her head. It was way too bright.

Then reality hit her.

She wasn't at home. She was in her cabin. The only other person here was Cooper.

And he was knocking on her door.

She shot upright and dragged her hand through her hair. Ever since he'd caught her staring at his package yesterday afternoon, she'd hardly been able to look him in the eye. It hadn't been too hard to keep out of his way, since she'd had to unpack. And when she'd driven to the local town for provisions, she had put her favorite rock band on full blast, which kind of killed any conversation stone dead.

It appeared Cooper had no intention of taking the hint and keeping his distance. Was it possible he hadn't seen her checking him out?

I wasn't checking him out. Her gaze had just sort of… slipped.

Besides, it wasn't as though he'd been entirely uninterested. Even now, hours later, the memory of his obvious erection straining against his jeans was enough to take her breath away.

"Hey, Paris." His sinfully sexy voice from the other side of the door was enough to cause goose bumps to chase over her bare arms. "You awake?"

Of course she was awake. She would have to be dead to sleep through the racket he was making.

"What do you want?" She sounded grouchy. She always sounded grouchy in the morning before her first cup of coffee.

"Open the door." It sounded like he gave it a kick. "Or I can come in. You decent?"

She stared at the door in disbelief. He really couldn't take a hint. On the plus side, perhaps it meant he hadn't seen her drooling yesterday. Come to think of it, she wasn't sure why she felt so awkward. If anything, *he* was the one who should be embarrassed. And clearly he wasn't.

"Yes, I'm decent." But as the door opened, panic hit her. Nobody ever saw her first thing in the morning, before she'd even had time to wipe the sleep from her eyes. Image was everything. She'd had that drummed into her from the moment she'd signed her first contract at the age of twelve. Even Hudson fucking Bartholomew, the supposed love of her life, had only ever seen her once before she'd had the chance to make herself look presentable.

The look on his face had been more than enough to

convince her that guys simply didn't want to see her looking like her normal rumpled self. Even after spending the night with her. Even if they supposedly *loved her more than life itself,* all they really wanted was the image.

It was too late to stop Cooper coming in now. She tugged the sheet up to her chin. She wasn't sure why. The sleeveless cotton top she wore covered a lot more than some of the skimpy things she'd had to wear as Lola over the last couple of years, and unless she pulled the sheet over her head she hadn't exactly hidden herself.

Cooper entered the room carrying a tray. He'd brought her breakfast in bed? *Seriously?*

With a flourish he placed the tray across her lap. There was a plate of pancakes, a quarter glass of orange juice and—thank God—a mug of coffee.

"There was no juicer," he said as he sat at the end of her bed as if this was a perfectly normal morning for them both. "I had to hand-squeeze those oranges."

She looked back down at the glass before he could see the stunned disbelief in her eyes. She hadn't thought twice when he'd bought the bag of oranges yesterday. He'd bought them so she could have freshly squeezed orange juice?

He really was taking his bodyguard duties above and beyond.

She cleared her throat. "I didn't know you could cook." He was built, he was sexy as hell, *and* he could cook. Did he have a girlfriend?

"Yeah, I can cook." He sounded amused that she might think otherwise. Would he find it funny when he discovered she didn't have a clue when it came to the kitchen? They'd ordered takeout yesterday and brought it home to eat. She'd planned to survive on fruit and salad. He didn't look as though he could survive on salad.

"Well, thanks." The aroma of the coffee made her fingers twitch. She couldn't live without her coffee and had brought her own machine with her. "Aren't you having any?"

He grinned. His hair looked damp and a shower fresh scent vied with the coffee for her attention. What time had he gotten *up*?

He looked good enough to eat. She dragged her fingers through her hair again, and by the feel of things she had a horrific case of bedhead. Inside she cringed—until she forcibly reminded herself that he was highly unlikely to take a photo of her looking like a witch and sell it to the highest bidder.

Of course he won't. He was Scott's best friend. *Even so…*

"I've already eaten. I thought I'd let you sleep in for a while."

He called seven a.m. on a non-work day *sleeping in*? With difficulty, she untangled her fingers from her hair and attempted to find some dignity. "Thank you."

She waited for him to take the hint and leave. Instead, he leaned back against the brass rails at the foot of her bed. Did he intend to watch her eat? Nerves spiked in the pit of her stomach as she picked up her cup and took a reviving gulp of coffee.

"No problem."

She peered at him over her steaming cup and tried to unscramble her brain. She looked hideous first thing in the morning, but this didn't appear to bother him. Of course, she hadn't just spent the night with him, which might account for it. On the other hand, there was a definite spark between them, which meant he found her hot.

At least, he'd found her hot yesterday when he'd brought her luggage in. She refused to let her gaze slip southwards now. Not that she'd see anything in any case, given the way he was sitting.

She squeezed her eyes shut and almost managed to convince herself the heat coursing through her was due entirely to the coffee flooding her system and absolutely nothing to do with Cooper Grayson and his dimple.

Cooper couldn't tear his gaze away from Paris. He'd known it was a mistake, bringing her breakfast in bed, but he'd set himself up to the dare, and thought he could handle it.

Seeing her in bed, all messy-haired and sleepy-eyed, was giving him ideas that only belonged in the dead of night. Was it because he knew she was strictly off-limits? He'd found other girls hot before now without following through into a wild night of frenzied fucking.

Hadn't he?

Whatever. None of them had been the sister of a friend, and when Scott had called last night, checking that everything was okay, he'd been forcibly reminded of that.

Not that it made much difference. Even if she hadn't been Scott's sister, and he hadn't been hired to protect her this week, she was way out of his league.

She was giving him a wary look. He could either leave her to eat, which was the rational option, or continue this weird-ass conversation.

He'd never been one for rational. In any case, there was something that had been bugging him ever since Scott had asked for this favor.

"If you wanted to buy a place to get away from it all, why'd you pick somewhere so close to home?"

Her nose twitched. He couldn't figure out whether it was because of his question or the steam from the coffee.

"It's easy to drive here if I just want to get away without flying somewhere."

As she spoke, her fingers tightened around the sheet she still held. Why was she clutching it to her throat like that? Christ, she wasn't naked was she?

His dick stirred. Fuck, he hadn't been this horny since he was a teenager. It didn't help knowing she felt the same way.

At least, that's what he'd thought when she'd given him that sexy once over yesterday afternoon. Then she'd gone all frosty for the rest of the day, barely answering him when he'd spoken and acting as though they didn't know each other in the grocery store. He hadn't managed to squeeze in a single *babe*. As soon as they'd arrived back at the cabin, she'd plugged in her earphones to eat their takeout before disappearing into her room.

It was only now, as he saw the defensive way she clutched both her mug and her sheet, that an entirely different thought occurred to him. Heat seared through him. Fuck. She didn't think he was trying to hit on her, did she?

He had to clear things up with her. He racked his brain to come up with something completely ordinary to say, with no sexual overtones at all. Surprisingly, the answer came to him without any trouble.

"Since we're here for the week I can do some work in

the yard for you. Might as well earn my keep." He offered her a mocking smile. Scott had insisted he pay his going rate, even though Cooper had told him where he could stuff the money. In the end, Scott had been persuaded to accept a discount, but it still stung.

Paris blinked her long, black lashes. His grim determination to look at her as nothing more than a kid sister died in a blaze of despicable lust. "Some work in the yard?" she echoed, as though she had no idea what he was talking about.

"It's a mess. When I'm not fighting off the paparazzi, I'll give it a makeover."

She still appeared to be having trouble processing his comment.

"But why would you want to do that? I'm pretty sure that's not part of the job description Scott gave you."

"What's that got to do with it? You're like the little sister I never had. Can't a brother help out without getting grilled?"

That was his cue to leave her bedroom, but before he could put his escape plan into action, a delicate blush spread over her cheeks. It stopped him in his tracks.

"Okay." Her voice sounded strangled. She dropped her gaze to her plate of rapidly cooling pancakes. "I hadn't planned on starting on the yard yet, but why not? I have some ideas for it. If you're sure you don't mind."

"I don't mind getting down and dirty for you." Well, shit. Why couldn't he ever think before he opened his big mouth? Sure, the comment could be taken to mean nothing more than backyard mud. Except the way she licked her lips and still refused to meet his gaze told him she'd instantly jumped to a different conclusion.

You wish.

"I'll see what I can come up with." Her voice was husky, and so damn sexy that all his good intentions gave him the bird and flew through the door.

Bringing her breakfast in bed hadn't been one of his best ideas. He wouldn't be doing it again. With difficulty, he eased himself off her bed.

"Look forward to it." As he reached the door, he couldn't resist glancing over his shoulder. She was looking at him, and there was no hint of the ice princess from the previous evening. Instead she smiled at him, and he didn't know whether it was because her hair was all messy and she still had a sleepy glow about her, but that smile kicked him right in the gut.

He closed the door and leaned against it as he took a deep breath. No way was he entering her bedroom again until it was time to move her luggage. He just hoped taming the jungle she called a backyard would leave him so exhausted that by the time he fell into bed, all he'd be good for would be passing out.

Like that was going to happen.

Chapter Three

Paris peered into the small mirror in the bathroom. It was steamed up, like the rest of the room, and she rubbed a circle clear with a corner of her towel.

Her mom would pitch a fit if she saw how basic this bathroom was. The shower had run hot and cold at random intervals, and only as she stepped out from the shower had she noticed the large spider that had been watching her from the ceiling.

She'd nearly screamed before she realized Cooper would probably break down the door to see what had happened. For some reason she didn't want him to know she was scared of creepy crawly things. *And I really don't want him seeing me dripping wet from the shower.* She eyed the spider. It didn't look as though it was about to pounce on her.

Of course, she hadn't planned to actually *stay* at the cabin until it was all done up. She'd bought it so she'd have a little getaway within easy reach of Beverly Hills, but without being in the spotlight.

But when the perfect opportunity to tell her mom she needed time on her own to think had dropped into her lap—more like burned her eyeballs, ugh—who was she to complain about a little hardship? Her mom had been so mortified at being caught *in the act* with Paris's last bodyguard, Anson, she'd hardly raised a word of protest.

Paris tried to block the vision from her mind. It was bad enough to discover her mom still had sex. It was pretty horrifying to know her mom had been screwing her bodyguard.

But all of that faded into insignificance at the actual sight of the pair of them going at it like desperate eighteen-year-olds. There should be a law against it or something.

She pulled a disgusted face at her reflection. The affair had been top secret. Not even her brother knew about it, and Scott knew about most things that went on at home. Since he'd been telling her for over a year that she needed to sort out her head, he'd been only too happy to help her misdirect their mom so she could escape for a few days.

Except her head was sorted. She didn't have to think about what she wanted to do with her life. She already knew.

She just had to find the right moment to tell her mom. And time was running out.

I could just fire her. People fired their managers all the time—but this was her *mom*. It wasn't that easy.

She'd answered a few of her mom's frantic messages with texts, telling her she was fine and not to worry. Although it seemed her mom was more concerned about Paris pissing off influential producers than the possibility she'd been permanently traumatized by catching her own mother doing unspeakable acts.

She shoved the nightmarish images to the back of her mind and dragged her fingers through her wet hair. If she were alone she'd just scrape it back into a band and be done with it. But she wasn't alone. Cooper was here.

Betraying warmth stole through her body. Yes, Cooper was here, and she found him even more irresistible this morning than she had yesterday. She'd half hoped he'd get her unspoken message that she didn't want them getting friendly, but obviously he didn't get subtle.

And she had to be honest—she'd felt like a right bitch giving him the cold shoulder when they went out yesterday. It wasn't as though he'd done anything to deserve it.

Apart from getting a massive hard-on.

Well, that could happen to guys for all sorts of reasons. She couldn't hold that against him.

I wouldn't mind holding him against me.

She blew out a long breath. It had been almost two years since she and Hudson fucking Bartholomew had split up. Which meant, despite what the tabloids said, it had been almost two years since she'd gotten laid.

It was very inconvenient that the first guy she'd wanted so badly since Hudson happened to be the one guy she shouldn't touch with a barge pole. Messing around with her brother's best friend was wrong on so many levels that she didn't know where to begin.

But it wasn't her overactive hormones that had her melting all over her bed as Cooper had left her room earlier. It was the way he so obviously was trying not to act on the magnetism between them.

She knew when a guy was attracted to her. Without fail, they came onto her with some cheesy line or other.

Cooper had offered to help tame her backyard.

He'd even thrown out that line about her being the little sister he'd never had. And the look in his eyes had been so far from *brotherly* it was a wonder she hadn't spontaneously combusted.

This week was going to test her acting abilities to their limit if she had to pretend to feel nothing but sisterly affection for him. On the other hand, how amazingly cool was it that he didn't seem to care at all about her Hollywood career? He really was treating her as if she were simply Scott's younger sister.

She couldn't remember the last time that had happened. Well, that was a lie. It had been ten years ago, before her mom had landed Paris's first contract. And the boy treating her that way had been...

Cooper Grayson.

Cooper was in the front yard finishing the daily maintenance on his souped-up Harley when he had the weirdest feeling of being watched.

He swung to find Paris leaning against the front doorframe, cradling a mug.

"Hi." Her smile did embarrassing things to his body. Did she have any idea how sexy she looked in those cut-off shorts and plaid shirt? "I brought you a coffee." She offered him the mug she held.

"Thanks." A cold beer would go down better, but it wasn't even nine in the morning and that was too early, even for him. He strolled over to her and took a reviving hit of caffeine and tried not to inhale the faint scent of oranges that wafted from her on the warm July breeze.

"The pancakes were yummy," she said, folding her arms, which had the distracting result of pushing up her breasts. *Not that he noticed.*

"Glad you enjoyed them."

"I was thinking you could teach me how to make them."

Was she joking? She didn't look as if she was. "They were just pancakes. I didn't do anything special." Although the kitchen looked like a mismatched nightmare, he'd had no trouble getting the battered old stove to work. In fact, it was in better condition that the one in the house where he and his brothers had grown up.

"Is that a no, you don't want to show me how to make pancakes?" Her smile turned challenging.

"Will I regret it?" He took another mouthful of coffee.

"I hope not." She was the picture of innocence as she gazed at him with those big green eyes of hers. "I've been told I'm a quick learner."

He choked on the coffee. Thank fuck it hadn't squirted out his nose. "You're a quick learner in the kitchen?"

Her lips parted and formed a seductively pink pout. There was no way in hell she wasn't doing that on purpose. "I don't know, Cooper. I've never had any instruction in the kitchen before."

He had the sudden image of her wearing nothing but a lacy French maid's apron, bent over the kitchen table, displaying her cute, naked ass.

His for the taking.

He only just stopped himself from groaning out loud. It was hard enough keeping his distance as it was. It was going to be fucking torture if she decided to show off her lethal flirtation techniques for the rest of the week.

But he wasn't going to let her get away with it unchallenged. He offered her one of the slow grins that Ella, who worked at *Grayson's*, his brothers' security company and really was like the sister he'd never had, told him could melt a frigid virgin's chastity belt at twenty paces.

"You sure you don't want me to show you what we could do with melted chocolate, champagne, and strawberries?"

The tip of her tongue peeked between her lips. He had the oddest notion she had no idea she was doing it. He found that even more of a turn on than her previous flirting.

"Doesn't seem like there's much skill involved with that."

"You'd be surprised. There's an art to melting chocolate." Not that he had a clue. He'd never melted chocolate in his life before, but the look of fascination on her face was worth any mockery he might suffer from his two brothers if this conversation ever got back to them.

"Well." She appeared to consider his remark. Her pupils were so huge the green had all but vanished. What the fuck was he doing here? Playing with fire, that's what. He couldn't seem to stop himself. "We don't have any chocolate."

He stared at her, and at the exact same moment that he laughed, so did she.

"You won't get out of it that easily. I have a bike and I know where the nearest grocery store is."

"Who says I want to get out of it? We should go buy some right now so you can't change your mind."

"On the bike?" His mocking challenge was out before he could stop himself. Having Paris cling to him as he rode through the mountains was an even worse idea than taking her pancakes in bed.

"Sure." Her answer was breezy. "Your bike doesn't scare me. I had to ride heaps when they had Lola dating a BDSM-obsessed biker for last Christmas' cliffhanger episode."

He knew she played a sexy character called Lola in *Sunset Heights*, but he'd never really watched the show.

"BDSM?" He hoped he didn't sound too keen. BDSM had never interested him. It gave him flashbacks to when he was a kid and his drunken father would pull out his belt to give him a thrashing—hardly a memory he wanted to surface when getting naked with a girl.

She smiled sweetly. It was nothing like the smile she'd given him earlier, but it was still a knockout. "The cliffhanger won awards. Though my favorite negative review said '*Sunset Heights fails to deliver on its promised porn*'. Cool, huh?"

"If you say so." *Soap opera and porn?* He'd have to check out that episode later. "You might want to change into jeans."

"I'll be five minutes. I need to change my hair as well."

He snorted. That was a new one. "Take your time." Then he couldn't resist. "Babe."

Chapter Four

Paris took the spare helmet Cooper offered her and matched the mocking grin he threw her way. There was no way in hell she was going to tell him her stunt double had been the one doing the scenes on the bike, and the closest she'd gotten to roaring along a deserted beach as the sun sank beyond the horizon was the green screen in the studio.

Her mom had ensured Paris's contract didn't allow her to do anything that might endanger her. She was only looking out for her but the problem was she didn't seem to realize Paris was now capable of making her own decisions.

Except, deep in her heart, she knew that wasn't true. It was more that her mom didn't *want* her making her own decisions.

In the spring last year she'd been accepted into Brown to study Liberal Arts. Her mom had never seen any problem with private tutors and home schooling to fit around Paris's work commitments, but for years she'd clung to the dream of going to college to finish her education. She wanted the freedom of attending classes that *she'd* chosen, and the experience of mixing with other students. Basically she just wanted a life that didn't revolve around her acting.

Her mom had persuaded her to defer for a year, and after that one conversation, they'd never mentioned it again.

A couple of weeks ago she'd shot her final episode of *Sunset Heights*. Everyone on the show had to sign nondisclosures. That was how much the network wanted to keep Lola's shock departure under wraps.

The relief was amazing. Another year of playing Lola and she might just've lost her mind.

The only problem was, her mom seemed to have completely forgotten about Brown.

"Here." Cooper handed her a pair of biking gloves. They looked a lot smaller than the ones he was pulling on his own hands.

"You carry spares with you?" She tugged on the leather gloves. They were pretty cool. "Girl-size spares?"

"I always like to be prepared." He flung her another of his wicked smiles and she pulled a face at him.

"Spare helmet, spare gloves. Anything else you have tucked away I should know about?"

"That would be telling."

She shook her head in mock disgust. "I can imagine."

"Hey, there's nothing wrong with being prepared."

She fell into step beside him as they made their way to his bike. It looked bigger than ever now that she was going to be riding it.

"I'm sure the bike they used on the show was smaller than this."

"Do you need a hand getting your leg over?" He leered at her in such an over-the-top way she laughed.

"No thanks. I'm perfectly able to get my leg over by myself." Right on cue she imagined swinging her leg over Cooper. They were naked. Of course. She smothered a sigh at her lack of control, swallowed her trepidation, and recalled the instructions she received last year on how to mount a bike.

A bike. Not a man. She gritted her teeth and waited until he'd pulled on his helmet and was in position before she jammed her own helmet on her head and followed those instructions with flawless precision. She didn't even need to clutch his tempting body to keep her balance. Instead, she gripped the handle behind her and sat up straight so she wasn't touching him at all.

He twisted round. His visor was still up and she tried not to focus on his come-to-bed-eyes. Not that she succeeded.

"You okay?" His voice came through her earpiece, sounding sinfully intimate. "Feel free to wrap your arms around me if you need to. I won't mind."

"I bet you won't." *Neither would she.* But it wasn't going to happen, because she had the terrible fear that if she wrapped her arms around him, he might guess she wasn't just flirting because there was a spark between them. She was flirting so he wouldn't guess how desperately she wanted to drag him off to bed.

He tapped his visor down. That she could no longer see his face didn't help at all. Then he lowered her visor, and it was beyond crazy the way her breath stalled in her chest at the almost-but-not-quite contact of his gloved finger.

When he finally turned around, she let out a silent sigh of

relief and relaxed her death grip on the handle. Excitement bubbled in the pit of her stomach. She had the feeling she was in for the ride of her life.

Cooper hit the road at a less breakneck speed than if he was riding alone. He always did when he had a girl ride pillion, but every other girl had plastered herself to his back and hugged him in a rib-crushing grip.

He'd been hoping Paris would do the same. Although it was probably just as well she didn't, seeing as it was hard enough to concentrate just knowing she was right behind him.

He checked his mirrors. There was nothing on the road. He'd seen no suspicious activity first thing that morning when he'd given the area a good sweep through his binoculars while she was still in bed. The gossip on the online tabloid sites was that Paris O'Connell had fled to Europe to recover from collapsing on set four days ago. If anyone was that desperate to get a sly shot of her, they'd be in London by now.

He wasn't taking any chances.

He didn't go to the same town as the day before. He parked in the lot behind the grocery store and scanned the area. Like the previous day, tourists overran this place, too. He pulled off his helmet and waited for Paris to slide off his bike before joining her. She flipped up her visor and then shifted as though she was uncomfortable.

"You okay?" The trip had only been forty minutes, but maybe he should have taken a break halfway.

"I'm fine. My butt's kind of numb, though."

He'd been trying not to think about her butt. Before he could stop himself the words were out there: "Want me to take a look?"

She wrinkled her nose. He wasn't sure whether that was because she was trying not to laugh or the thought of him checking out her butt didn't fill her with the same happy thoughts as it did him.

"I'll pass." She eased off the helmet. He didn't know what kind of glue she'd used, but her wig didn't budge an inch. "God, this wig makes me so hot."

He almost told her she didn't need the wig to make her hot, but this time managed to curb his tongue. Shame he hadn't learned that trick years ago. It would've saved him a shitload of trouble with his old man.

He fixed the helmets to his bike. "I'll get the champagne. You sort out the chocolate and strawberries." Not that he had any intention of leaving her side, but whatever. He also needed to get some provisions. They'd only bought rabbit food the day before.

She pushed her sunglasses up her nose with one finger. "I don't drink champagne." There was a defensive note in her voice, as though she expected him to laugh. He eyed her as they made their way to the main road. She was looking dead ahead.

He wasn't sure why she'd gone all prickly. Not everyone liked champagne. He'd only had it once and couldn't figure out what all the fuss was about. "What's your poison then?"

She shrugged. "Depends how I feel."

"Like to keep your options open, huh?"

"That's right. It's my choice."

He was definitely all for choice. When he was eight, his older brother Alex had caught him stealing one of their dad's beers. Alex had held him down and made him drink the whole damn bottle. Cooper had vomited the rest of the night, but he'd learned his lesson.

He hadn't touched beer again until he'd turned twelve, in a futile attempt to drown his guilt over Alex being arrested. All his brother had been doing was trying to save Cooper's ass from their dad's drunken fury.

He soon learned beer didn't drown anything. Instead, the fear had hit him that he'd turn into his father. It was enough to scare the crap out of him.

Sure, he'd hung around the back streets as a teen, drinking and smoking shit, but unlike his friends, he'd known when to stop tipping the booze down his throat. While they'd been crawling in the gutter with killer hangovers, he'd been the bookie for his other brother Jackson's illegal street fighting operation.

His choices might've given the welfare people a seizure if they'd known about them, but the fact was, they were his choices to make.

W hy had she told Cooper she didn't drink champagne? Paris tucked her thumbs into the pockets of her jeans and refused to look at him. Just because she hadn't been able to stomach alcohol since leaving rehab didn't mean she wanted anyone to know that.

It was easy to pretend to drink at the parties and endless glitzy functions she went to. It was all about being seen with the right people at the right time. At least by being sober she never ended up in the tabloids for flashing her thong in public.

She figured it would be a lot harder to fool Cooper when it was just the two of them together in that tiny cabin. Except now he'd gone quiet, and that was so unlike him. He probably imagined she was being some kind of drama queen.

She'd certainly drank anything that was offered to her when she'd been sixteen, but she didn't want to remember what a mess she'd been at sixteen, because it only reminded her that when she'd split up with Hudson a few years later, the thought of drowning her sorrows had made her physically sick.

"Lemonade could work."

She stopped dead and turned to look at him. "*What*?"

He flashed his dimple at her. She really wished he wouldn't. "You do know I don't have a fucking clue what to do with chocolate, strawberries, and champagne, right? I mean are we supposed to pour it into the chocolate as it melts or what? Why waste good money? Lemonade might work."

He didn't think she was being a diva at all. She had the scary urge to wrap her arms around his neck. She managed to contain herself. "Sure, we can try that."

He shoved his hands into his pockets and nodded across the street. "Want to stop off here?"

She barely glanced at the coffee shop. "Sounds good."

He found them a table in the shade of a cottonwood and instead of sitting opposite her, sat next to her. "We're undercover, right?" he said, as he leaned in as though he was about to kiss her.

Her stomach fluttered, even though he was just doing it for show. "That's right," she agreed.

"So, if I do this…" He casually slid his arm around her shoulders. "You're not going to knee me in the balls, are you?"

She flattened her sweaty palms on her thighs and refused to peek where his balls resided. "Wouldn't dream of it." Shit, she sounded as though her throat was congested.

A waitress came to their table and flipped open her notepad. "What can I get you?" Her gaze drifted past Paris and settled on Cooper. Her perfunctory smile brightened by about a hundred watts. Paris bit her lip to stop herself from giggling. Cooper appeared unaware of the interest he'd stirred.

"What do you want, babe?" He offered her a wicked grin, daring her to respond in kind. She wanted to, but suppose the waitress recognized her voice? She slid the laminated menu across the table and jabbed her finger at the iced chocolate.

Cooper gave their order. "Want anything to nibble on?" His voice dripped with false innocence. She shook her head and let out a relieved breath when the waitress finally sauntered away.

"I don't think we raised any suspicions." He wound a length of her wig around his finger. She couldn't feel a thing. Now, if only he was doing that to her *real* hair. She tried, without much conviction, to shove that thought aside.

He's only doing it for show. Right?

"She wasn't interested in me at all." Since he was clearly comfortable with the whole playacting aspect of their outing, she shifted closer to him on the bench until their thighs touched. She'd have never guessed she was into masochism before, but why else was she torturing herself this way? "She couldn't take her eyes off you, though."

Was it her imagination or did his hold around her shoulders tighten?

"Jealous, babe?"

She laughed, and then slapped her hand across her mouth. Since nobody glanced their way, she relaxed and patted his denim covered thigh in what she hoped was a condescending manner. *Was that even possible?*

"I don't get jealous, bunny." God, his muscles were rock hard.

He tugged her closer. That definitely wasn't her imagination—and had she really left her hand on his thigh? Her fingers twitched, but she still didn't move her hand. It wasn't as though she was pushing boundaries. After all, her hand was nearer his knee than his balls.

"Good. Nothing worse than a jealous girlfriend."

An earlier thought came back to haunt her, and she snatched her hand from his leg. "Do you have a girlfriend?"

Despite having wondered about it, somehow she'd assumed he hadn't. She had to remember that while Cooper might flirt like a pro, he hadn't hit on her and had made it clear he had no intention of doing so. She'd put that down entirely to his friendship with Scott, but suppose there was more to it than that?

It was annoying that the idea of him having a girlfriend kind of pissed her off.

"Me?" He laughed as though she'd just cracked a joke. "Not likely. Who'd want to take me on?"

Paris ignored the warm glow that surged through her at the knowledge he wasn't seeing anyone special. It made no difference at all.

Much.

"Looking for compliments?" She very nearly mauled his thigh again, but managed to resist. "Don't tell me you live the life of a monk. I bet you have girls dying to be your one and only."

His fingers dropped from her wig and idly caressed her shoulder through the short-sleeved shirt she was wearing. It was crazy the way he made her feel. She couldn't remember being this wired—even the first time she'd met Hudson.

"Not once they get to know me." His lazy grin did something wet and wonderful way down low, but there was an odd tension in his words.

"You're that bad, huh?" There was a husky note in her voice. God help her.

"I've had my moments."

Without warning she was plunged into the past, to before her mom had uprooted her and Scott from everything and everyone they'd ever known. Her mom had hated the way Scott hung out with Cooper and flatly forbade her to go anywhere near any of those Grayson boys, who were nothing but trouble.

Paris knew, some time when she was ten, Cooper had ended up in the ER, though it was a couple of years later before she understood the reason why. Not that she saw why her mom felt vindicated in trying to keep Scott away from his best friend. How was it his fault that his father had beaten the crap out of him?

There in the coffee shop, she couldn't stop the shiver that

raced over her arms. She'd never known her own dad, and while her mom drove her insane half the time, she would never raise a finger to hurt her.

She couldn't even begin to imagine how he must feel about his father. It was a wonder Cooper hadn't ended up in jail or something. She had a terrible urge to ask him about that time, but she never would.

It was a relief when the waitress brought their order, along with another dazzling smile in Cooper's direction. It was kind of rude. For all the other girl knew, they might be involved. In fact, he still had his arm around her so that they would appear to be a couple.

She was desperately tempted to run her fingers along his jaw and say something extremely nauseating before giving the waitress a triumphant smirk.

Except if the waitress recognized her then all her plans for hiding away this week would sink. If it got out where she was, her mom was sure to hear about it.

She really didn't want to face her mom just yet.

Gritting her teeth, she held her tongue. The waitress eventually sauntered off, swinging her butt in an entirely un-necessary way.

"What about you?"

She frowned at him. He was obviously continuing their conversation but she had no idea what he was referencing. "How do you mean?"

"Boyfriend? Someone special? It's only fair, I answered you."

For a couple of seconds Cooper didn't think she was going to answer him. She might be dating some big Hollywood star. Although, if that were the case he had the feeling Scott might've mentioned it at some point. He'd certainly had a lot to say about the scumbag who'd broken Paris's heart a couple of years back.

"I'm not seeing anyone." She took a long suck on her straw, and he had the sudden, gut-punching vision of her wrapping those pink lips around his dick.

He shifted on the hard bench, but it didn't ease his inconvenient erection. Dragging his mind from his pants, he focused on her answer.

He found the fact she wasn't seeing anyone hard to believe. "No one serious, you mean?" Then again, what did he know about getting serious? He ran a mile if a girl he'd slept with just wanted to hang out. Sex was never serious. He always made that clear upfront. That might make him shallow, but at least he owned it.

She pulled the straw from her mouth in a long, slow slide, and then licked her lips. His thoughts instantly dived south again.

"I have dates with guys," she said, as she traced patterns on the battered timber table. "But that's as far as it goes. It's mostly for publicity."

"No secret lover the press doesn't know about?"

A smile tugged at her lips, and she turned to look at him. He wished she'd take those sunglasses off so he could see her gorgeous eyes.

"Wouldn't be a secret if I told you, would it?"

He trailed his fingertips along the smooth skin of her arm and she gave a delicate shudder.

She's off-limits.

But he still couldn't pull his hand away.

"So you're not using this week as a time out from an intense relationship?" His brothers would piss themselves if they ever heard him using the word *relationship*. Neither of them thought he knew the meaning of the word.

A pensive expression flashed over her face, as though he'd hit a raw nerve. Did that mean she was seeing someone? He wasn't sure why the thought rubbed him the wrong way.

"If you must know…" She sounded reluctant to share, and focused on her drink, stabbing her straw through the swirl of cream. "I needed time away from my mom. And my bodyguard."

Scott had told him about her firing the bodyguard, but he didn't know why.

As for her mom, she had never sworn or shouted at him, and had always been unfailingly polite, but even as a kid he'd known he didn't meet her high standards. She hadn't liked the way he and Scott had always hung out together. She'd probably bust an artery if she knew who Paris was spending this week with.

"Your mom can be kind of high maintenance." How was that for diplomacy?

Paris gave a snort of laughter. "You remember her, then?"

"Hard to forget."

She let out a long sigh. "You can say that again. Don't get me wrong. When we first started out she kept the sharks away when they thought she'd be a pushover. Ha! They soon learned the error of their ways."

He could imagine. Cora O'Connell was a prime example

of a momager from hell.

"So, you're just slumming it this week as a break from your mom before you hit the high life again?"

The way her lips thinned told him she didn't think much of his remark.

"No, *actually*." She sounded irritated. "I'm considering my options."

He took a long swallow of his iced coffee and casually glanced around. No one appeared to be taking undue notice of them—although he didn't like the look of the guy lounging by the corner of the coffee shop. Not that there was anything especially suspicious about him, or the way he was drinking his coffee and scrolling through his cell.

He turned back to Paris. "What options? Do they give you options on what happens in the soap?"

She spluttered into her drink. "Yeah, right." Then she looked at him, and he was certain if she wasn't wearing the huge shades, and her bangs didn't cover her forehead, he'd see her frowning big time. "That would be a no, Cooper."

He shrugged and managed not to grin, since he didn't think his amusement would go down well. Trouble was, she was so damn cute when she was pissed off.

"So, your options are state secrets that you can't reveal." This time he couldn't stop the grin, and after a moment where she glared at him, she finally let out a huff and shook her head.

"It's no big deal. I'm just thinking what direction I want"—she hesitated for a second—"my career to head in, that's all."

"Had enough of *Sunset Heights*?"

"I've been on that show for over ten years." He heard

a thread of frustration in her voice, and she waved her arm in a dismissive gesture he recalled from years ago. From the corner of his eye he saw the guy he'd noticed earlier glance in their direction. "It's time I looked at other things."

"I'm not arguing." He picked up his glass and drained the contents while he gave the guy another once-over. He was back to reading on his cell.

"I've had a couple of callbacks for a movie role." There was an oddly defensive note in her voice, and at any other time he'd probe into that. But the guy with the cell was edging toward them in a decidedly furtive manner.

With his arm still around her, Cooper cradled her face with his free hand. *Damn, her skin was soft.* She looked at him, her lips parted in obvious astonishment, and it was hard to remember the only reason he was here was because he had a job to do.

He leaned in close. Her uneven breath was distracting. He swallowed, and his lips brushed hers. "*Keep looking at me.*"

"What?" Her whisper branded his lips. He grazed her cheek with his jaw and found her ear, half hidden beneath that damn wig.

"Don't turn around. Focus on me. I think we have a tail."

She went rigid—but she didn't turn around. "What are you going to do?"

He pulled her to her feet and tucked her against his side, shielding her from Cell Man. "Get you out of here."

Chapter Five

Paris smothered the flare of resentment that, yet again, her personal life was being invaded. It didn't do any good. Why couldn't she just enjoy some downtime without being hounded?

Head down, she let Cooper take the lead. So much for her week of anonymity. She steeled her nerves for the inevitable confrontation between Cooper and whoever had been trying to sneak a photo of her.

No chance of keeping things under the radar now. He might stop the one suspicious person with some heavy threats, but he couldn't keep everyone else from taking photos on their cells.

It happened every time.

He strolled with apparent nonchalance toward the street. He didn't seem to be at the point of shoving her behind his back while he did a macho bodyguard face-off thing.

She edged closer to him, and his body heat sent whirlpools

of sensation through her. It was hard to remember what she wanted to ask him.

"Where are we going?" It was a breathy whisper as she scanned the area in front of them. She couldn't see any suspicious activity, and she was pretty paranoid when it came to suspicious activity.

"For a ride." He slung her a bone-melting smile, but she had the feeling that behind those shades he was looking over her shoulder.

She squashed the urge to glance back to see who he was looking at. The strangest thought had occurred to her.

"You mean you're not going to tell them to back off?"

This time when he looked at her she knew his entire attention really was on her. "I thought you didn't want to draw attention to yourself."

"Well, no." Flustered by his reaction, and not quite sure why, she focused on his bike as they crossed the lot. "But I mean, that's your job. To confront them and tell them where they can shove their cameras."

She felt his big body shake in silent laughter. "Yeah, and then the whole town would know you're here. This way there's only the possibility that one sleazy guy suspects."

Paris watched him unlock the helmets from his bike. She was still trying to grapple with his reasoning, which so closely mirrored her own. "All my other bodyguards always confront them." Her mom practically made it a requirement of the job. *Let one paparazzo get away with it, and they'll be swarming over you like flies.*

Which meant any incognito night out she planned invariably turned into a circus—and ended up with her photo splashed across gossip magazines.

Instead of handing her the helmet, he slowly slid it over her head. "That's not my M.O., Paris."

The way he said her name, all dark and sexy, turned her legs to jelly. He pulled on his own helmet, and his voice came through her earpiece.

"He's followed us. His bike isn't any match for mine. Just climb on real slow, like you don't give a shit." With that, he mounted his Harley. She glanced over her shoulder and caught sight of a guy strolling after them. He looked vaguely familiar. She took a deep breath, flicked down her visor, and followed Cooper in getting on the bike.

This time she wrapped her arms around his solid body. God, that felt good. She hardly even cared why they'd had to cut short their excursion, and that was a first. Usually by now she'd be freaking out inside, where no one could see, but that was because usually she'd be the center of attention, while her bodyguard flexed his muscles and acted like some kind of steroid enhanced Terminator.

Before she could stop herself, she ran her palms over Cooper's taut abs. She bet he didn't owe anything to steroids. The Harley roared to life, and leashed power throbbed through her body, igniting her nerve endings and centering between her thighs.

She swallowed her groan before he could hear it, and gripped him tighter as he took off in a rumble of thunder.

"Hang on tight." His smoky voice filled her head. "I'm going to lose this asshole."

Instead of the dull sense of despair that once again she'd been easy prey for some louse, excitement zapped through her. She clung tight as he'd instructed, and embraced the sense of danger that vibrated all around.

For an endless, exhilarating time, he raced along the mountain road. She knew, without him having to say, that they were definitely being followed. Awe threaded through her. She hadn't noticed anything while they'd been at the café. Usually she was hypersensitive about being watched. It seemed that being with Cooper was playing havoc with more than just her hormones.

Without warning he swerved off the road onto a rough trail, and she gasped soundlessly as the forest swallowed them. Was this even legal? She had no idea. Cooper wouldn't care.

They went deeper, until even the trail vanished. Trees loomed overhead and sunlight filtered through the green canopy, giving everything a surreal glow—and still he wove through the forest as though he knew exactly where he was going.

She didn't care where he was taking her. Beneath her hand his heart thudded. They were both fully clothed, and yet she felt closer to him than she had with Hudson the handful of times they had been naked.

She didn't want the ride to ever end.

And then he skidded to a stop, and she clutched his chest. Before them, a picture perfect creek swirled around boulders, creating sparkling rapids and glinting pools. Sycamores and alders dotted the shoreline, casting mystical shadows across the water. It looked like something from a fantasy movie.

"We should be safe here." Cooper's voice broke her reverie. "You okay?"

Okay didn't cover it. She was having trouble breathing, as though she'd just run a marathon. "Yeah, I'm great."

For a few seconds she just sat there with her arms around

him, hardly daring to move in case it broke this magical spell.

Finally he stirred, and with reluctance she unhooked her fingers from his T-shirt so he could dismount. He offered her his arm, and instead of pushing him aside, she held onto him as he helped her off the bike. Just as well, really. Her legs were wobbling like crazy.

He pulled off his gloves and helmet, and then, without asking, he unstrapped hers. His fingers brushed against her throat, and she held her breath in the vain hope that would slow her erratic heartbeat.

If anything, it made it worse.

Or better.

Whatever.

She tore off her own gloves and flung her arms around his neck. She distantly heard a thud as he dropped her helmet. Then his arms were around her and he held her close.

"Thank you." It was hard to speak, but she had to say something to account for the way she'd flung herself into his arms. For the way she was *still* in his arms. His biceps felt so much better than she'd imagined. She closed her eyes and savored the moment. It was wrong, though. It could never go anywhere.

So why does it feel so right?

"Just doing my job." His voice was rough against her ear. He appeared in no hurry to let her go. "Keeping you safe."

"Yes…" *I feel safe with you.* She sank against him. He was all corded muscle and leashed strength. *Don't let me go.*

He loosened his grip on her, and his body tensed. "Paris." His voice was gruff, and he scanned the forest around them.

Reality slammed through her, and she froze. *Is he looking for someone?* She slowly pulled back. *What am I doing?* They might've known each other years ago, but he was practically a stranger to her now.

Suppose he set this whole thing up, just to get me alone out here? Was that paparazzo somewhere out there, hiding behind a tree, waiting for the right moment to get a sleazy shot of her?

For endless seconds she stared at him as that horrible thought pounded through her mind. *He's Scott's best friend.* He wouldn't do that to her.

And there's no need for him to try and get me alone. They were alone in the cabin. And he'd made it very clear he wasn't going to take advantage of her. Why would he go to all this trouble, when he could easily set up a hidden camera in her bedroom?

"Hell. I didn't mean to—" He gave an awkward shrug. "It's just…"

"It's fine," she said quickly. "*I'm* fine."

I'm also seriously deranged if I think you want to get me naked in the middle of the forest just so that some low-life can take photos of me. She had to stop thinking the worst of people. At least, when it came to *him*. Her brother might be a dick on occasion, but he was no fool. Unlike *her*, he was a damn good judge of character.

"Are you sure?" Cooper's entire focus was on her now. It was unnerving. "I've customized the bike to go off road, but it was still a bumpy ride."

She had the crazy urge to laugh, but for once he didn't look as though he'd just cracked a joke. *Don't say it.* She couldn't stop herself. "Guess my ass will let me know in the morning, huh?"

He swallowed, as though the thought of her ass wasn't

so great. "We'll give it ten minutes and then leave. He'll be long gone by then."

"Okay." Her gaze slipped. His T-shirt stretched across impressive pecs and his arms—

Don't think about his arms. Except she couldn't help it. She wanted his arms around her again.

Stop drooling over him. He wasn't going to act on this insane attraction between them, and thank God for that. Because that would be a *disaster*.

She wracked her brains for something intelligent to say. "He'd be crazy to try and tangle with you, anyway."

Ugh…

"I won't let him near you."

"I know." It seemed the forest shrank around them, until there wasn't enough air to breathe properly. She hitched in a shallow gasp. All she had to do was reach out and they'd be touching.

Don't do it.

Her fingers trailed along the unyielding gorgeousness of his chest. Butterflies erupted in her stomach, and she took an unintentional step toward him.

"Paris, no." He gripped her hand, but instead of pushing her away, he held her there. "We can't do this. You know that."

"We're not doing anything."

God, his hands are so strong. She'd never found anything sexy about hands, but that was before Cooper.

His fingers tightened around hers. They were so close that his body heat wrapped around her like a velvet embrace. "You're Scott's little sister." He sounded as though that was the worst thing in the world.

She shuddered and breathed in deep. The scent of forest

and flowers swirled all around, but it was the exotic hint of nutmeg and citrus in Cooper's cologne that sank into her blood and set up a throbbing need deep in her sex.

Let go of him. He wouldn't try and stop her from moving away, but it was a distant demand, lost beneath the overwhelming reality of being plastered against his hard body.

He was hard all right.

Step back right now.

She couldn't.

"He'll never know." *Had she said that out loud?* She turned her head and slowly drifted her cheek along his jaw. His stubble grazed her like a rough caress.

"I'll know."

Is he going to make me beg? The crazy thing was, he wanted her. She knew it. And his refusal to instantly take what she offered just made him even more irresistible.

"Does it matter?" Her whisper was ragged. *Don't push me away.*

"He's my oldest friend. My best friend." He sounded agonized. "I can't betray his trust."

Is it wrong to find that such a turn on? There weren't many guys she knew who'd reject her for that reason.

Even so…

"This has got nothing to do with my brother. It's between you and me."

"I'm supposed to be looking out for you. Not—"

Her lips found his and silenced whatever else he might've said. For an endless moment neither of them moved, as though they were caught in an invisible web. Then she tugged her hands free and raked her fingers through his hair, the silken strands sliding over her palms.

He groaned, the sound vibrating through their joined lips, and one hand slid along her back to cup her ass.

"Cooper." She breathed his name against his mouth, and in answer he kissed her—a hot, demanding kiss that shattered forever any pretense that lust didn't sizzle between them.

She opened her mouth and his tongue slid inside. She rocked against him, wanting to be closer, needing him in a way that turned her mind inside out.

He pulled back, panting. "We need to stop."

Was he for real? She'd just had the best kiss of her life, and he thought they should *stop*?

"No, we don't."

"What the hell are we doing?"

It wasn't really a question. He didn't need an answer, and she didn't want to talk about it anymore.

She rolled onto her toes and nipped his bottom lip. *Distract him.* "You're the hottest bodyguard I've ever had."

He laughed and didn't back off, which had to be a good thing. "Had a few, have you?"

She trailed her fingernails along the back of his neck and he shuddered. God, that was a turn on. Despite her image, and all the hangers-on, she'd never felt this kind of power when it came to sex before, not even with Hudson.

"They don't last long with my mom watching their every move." *She wasn't going to think about Anson.* "Let me know if you're interested in a full-time position."

She didn't mean it—of course she didn't. Cooper was far too distracting to have around on a full-time basis. But it sure made for a tempting fantasy.

He hugged her so tight she was amazed he didn't crush

her bones. Breathing was overrated, anyway. "This an interview?" Without warning he pulled her wig off and forked his fingers through her hair. "You need my full résumé?"

She clutched his shoulders before her knees gave way. His smile was deadly.

"I guess I do." She sounded hoarse. "A girl can't be too careful."

He slid his hand beneath her shirt. Her knees gave up the fight and buckled. Luckily her fingers didn't have any intention of releasing their death grip on his shoulders. She swallowed a groan as he explored her naked back. He leaned in close and nipped the sensitive flesh beneath her ear.

"Tell me to stop." His husky growl was the sexiest thing ever.

He can't be serious. She tightened her grip on him. "Don't you dare stop."

"*Paris.*"

With a frustrated moan she dragged his shirt from his jeans. His flesh was warm and tautly muscled. She closed her eyes behind her shades, relieved he couldn't see just how much he affected her.

"Keep going. Full résumé, remember?"

He ground out a curse and tugged open her jeans. *Oh God, yes...*

"You sure about this?" His breath was hot against her face, but not as hot as his words. She writhed helplessly as he worked his fingers inside her panties, and nearly died when he touched her swollen clit.

She tried to say *yes* but it sounded more like a feral growl. He didn't appear to care.

"You're so wet." His finger slid along her and she

shuddered. Every beat of her heart pulsed between her thighs. She'd never felt anything like it before.

"Push my jeans down." She'd do it herself but she was afraid she might collapse if she let go of him. Why did he need telling in any case? Shouldn't he be ripping her clothes off her by now?

"I wish." His grip on her hair tightened, and he pushed one finger inside her. "Fuck, this is killing me."

She panted and squeezed his finger. *So good.* She needed more. "Cooper." She sounded like she was drowning.

His mouth on hers silenced her. His kiss was savage, and his finger teased her sensitive flesh, electrifying every nerve ending.

She let out a choked gasp, and he tore his mouth from hers.

"Can't take any chances." He massaged her slick flesh. Stars danced behind her eyes. "I'm not that well prepared."

She had no idea what he was talking about.

"*Please.*" She breathed the word against his mouth. She really *was* begging for it. Any other time she would've found the concept hysterical. "I want you."

He made a strangled sound in his throat. "I'm not a fucking saint."

Roughly he pulled her head to his shoulder. Without thinking, she sank her teeth into his neck. He bucked against her, and she licked his delicious skin as he cupped her sex in the palm of his hand.

They were plastered against each other. Cooper's hand was tight against her, constricted by her jeans. Her heart thundered, and she couldn't breathe. He buried his face in her hair and teased her clit as the world shattered around her.

It was forever before she could drag in more than a shallow gasp. As Lola she'd had more on screen lovers than she could remember. In real life, there'd only been Hudson, and while his foreplay technique was flawless—he'd told her so the night he took her virginity—she'd never been able to really let herself go.

There hadn't been a whole lot of foreplay with Cooper. Not that she'd needed it. From the second she'd seen him again, every moment had been one long slow burn. Even if she *had* spent half the time pretending to ignore him, her body hadn't been fooled for a second.

He was still holding her, one hand shoved between her legs when reality slapped her in the face.

She hadn't just come for the first time in her life. She'd done it *over his hand*.

"Damn, Paris." His throaty words pulled her back to the present. "That was the sexiest thing I've ever seen."

Her fingers twitched where she still clung onto his shoulders. "What was?" She sounded like an idiot.

He kissed her. A soft, hot kiss, that set off a chain reaction from her lips to her tender clit. His hand slid from her hair and cupped the back of her neck. "Watching you come."

Her legs wobbled. They seemed to do nothing else when she was around him. "Really?"

Shit, had she said that out loud? But instead of wanting to disappear into a hole in the ground, like she had a minute ago, she smiled at him. Because seriously, who wouldn't when Cooper Grayson said something like that to her?

His finger teased her sensitized clit as he slowly pulled his hand free. She tried not to shudder and completely failed. It was kind of shocking to realize she wanted to do it all over again already.

"Yeah, really." There was a strained note in his voice as he held the open fly of her jeans between his finger and thumb. "I just wish I'd been inside you. Except that might've blown my fucking mind."

She was still smiling at him. He probably thought she was totally goofy. And then the meaning behind his words hit her.

"Oh." She froze in the act of trailing her fingers over his jaw and glanced down. Cooper was still buttoned up, but his erection was obvious. Her heart sped up again and thumped against her ribs. "Why didn't you— I mean, don't you want to…"

Before she could embarrass herself any more, he rested his forehead against hers. "No condoms, babe."

I'm not that well prepared. So that's what he'd meant. She should've guessed.

Poor guy looked in agony. She slid her hand down his chest and abs and flattened her palm over his erection. God, he was big.

He gripped her wrist. "Don't."

"Why not?" She looked up at him. His dimple was no-where in sight. "Don't you like it?" She knew he did. She knew why he wanted her to stop, too. But that wasn't going to happen.

"I'm not coming when I can't be inside you."

She pressed her thighs together but it did nothing for the lust swirling through her. Instead she tightened her grip around him. "*I* did."

His groan was the best sound she'd ever heard. "That's different." But he didn't push her away. He angled her hand more securely over him. Ripples chased through her tender sex. She was *desperate* for him again. It was crazy.

She'd never teased a guy like this before. On set it was all choreographed, and she'd never been comfortable enough to do anything like this with Hudson. Which was weird, since she and Cooper weren't even really dating.

Maybe that was the difference. It was kind of exciting.

She rose onto her toes again and whispered in his ear. "That's kind of sexist."

He gripped her ass, grinding her against their joined hands. "I'm all for equality, but I'm not fucking coming in front of you."

She flexed her fingers around his rigid length and nibbled kisses along his jaw. He shuddered, and that exhilarating sense of power rushed through her again. She gripped his butt, mirroring how he held her, and wriggled against him for good measure.

"Wanna bet?"

"Paris." There was a warning in his voice, but mostly it was pure lust. He sure wasn't putting up much resistance, that was for sure. "Not going to happen."

"Okay." She let go of his butt and cupped his balls. He almost broke her goddamn wrist when his grip tightened. "Still want me to stop?" God, this was fun, in a kind of masochistic way.

"Yes." He ground the word between his clenched teeth. She gave him a little squeeze, just because she could, and he wrenched her off him with a muffled curse.

"Cooper." It was all she could manage, but he didn't answer. He just swung around, shoulders hunched, tension spiking from him.

She wound her arms around him and leaned her cheek against his back as he finished what she'd started. Time lost all meaning. All she could feel was Cooper's rigid body, until finally he let out a stifled groan and his muscles relaxed. But he didn't move, and neither did she, and slowly she became aware of the gurgling of the creek and the birdsong in the forest.

He took a deep breath, but still didn't look at her. "Christ." His voice shook. "That was insane."

"Mm." With reluctance she let go of him and fixed her jeans. Was he mad at her? She didn't know what to say, so she picked up her wig and focused on pulling out all the bits of twig and leaves that had caught in the hair.

He still didn't turn around. It was starting to freak her out. "Are you okay?" There was an edge in her voice.

"Sure." He tossed her an oddly brooding look over his shoulder then hunkered down at the edge of the creek to freshen up. She fiddled with her wig for a little longer before pulling on the leather gloves.

This was so much worse than after she'd first had sex with Hudson. He'd been smugly satisfied and assumed she was, too. This time it appeared *she* was the smugly satisfied one, because Cooper sure didn't give the impression he'd enjoyed himself.

She picked up her helmet and hugged it. What had she been thinking, pushing Cooper over the edge like that?

The one guy she'd met who didn't give a shit about her celebrity status, and she'd managed to screw it up within two days. At least he wouldn't sell the sordid tale to the press. She should be thankful for that.

Surely he wouldn't sell her out...would he?

Cooper forcibly unclenched his fists and stood. He'd been a fucking idiot, but he had to face Paris sooner or later. If he were her, he'd fire himself on the spot.

He turned round. She was clutching her helmet and biting her lip. He took a deep breath and went over to her.

"Hey." His voice was gruff, and the way she kind of angled her body away from him didn't help. He resisted the urge to cup her chin and make her look at him. "Look. That shouldn't have happened. It won't happen again."

Heat flared through him. It *wouldn't* happen again, but hell if he didn't want it to. Except, next time, he'd make damn sure he had an entire box of condoms handy.

There wasn't going to be a next time. She'd only turned to him because she'd been hyped up by the chase — not because she really wanted him. Why the hell would a girl like Paris want someone like *him*?

She didn't answer, unless he counted the shrug she gave him. She wasn't going to let him off the hook that easy, and he didn't blame her.

He was supposed to be protecting her, and for the last God knows how long all that had been on his mind was how fucking irresistible she was.

He cleared his throat. "It's no excuse, but we weren't followed. There's nobody here. We weren't seen."

She glanced up at him then, her pink lips parted. *Don't think about her lips.* He definitely wasn't going to think about how she'd fallen apart, clutching him as though he was the only thing in her world. It left every wet dream he'd ever had in the dust.

"Right." She nodded and shuffled a couple of steps back from him. "That…that's good. I, uh, was worried about that."

Guilt snaked through him. "I'm sorry." More than she'd ever know, and for more reasons than he would ever admit. "You want to get back home?"

"Mm." She nodded again and jammed the helmet over her head. He got on his bike, and she swung her leg over but didn't cling to him like she had before.

He told himself that was a good thing.

They passed nothing suspicious on the way back. At least he'd lost their tail. He attempted to whip up some anger against the bastard but couldn't, because if not for him, the mind blowing hookup with Paris would never have happened. No way would she have wrapped herself around him otherwise—and no matter what he told her, the truth was he couldn't regret a second of it.

Shit, this week was going to kill him.

B y the time they arrived at the cabin, Cooper had convinced himself he'd dodged a bullet. She hadn't gone crazy, which meant she was willing to overlook his unprofessional behavior. He sure as shit couldn't—not only because he was supposed to be watching out for her this week, but because she was Scott's little sister.

Before they'd even gotten off the bike, Scott's Kawasaki roared along the dirt road and into the front yard. Cooper stared in disbelief as Paris's brother dismounted and strolled toward them. Of all the times he had to turn up. It was like he knew Cooper had crossed the line.

"Hey." Scott pulled off his helmet and grinned. "How's it going?"

Fucking great. Cooper turned to give Paris a hand, but she managed without any help.

"Fine." She pulled off her own helmet and a sprinkle of leaves on the back of her wig drew his attention like a great big neon sign. "What're you doing here?"

"First, I wanted to make sure you hadn't trashed my car." Scott shot his SUV a pointed look. "And second, why haven't you answered any of my calls? I don't mean with text messages. You've been avoiding talking to me."

"That's right." She strolled to the front door as though nothing had happened between them. Some of Cooper's tension eased. Obviously heavy make out sessions in the forest weren't that big a deal to her. Strangely, that bugged him.

Paris continued, "What makes you think I want to talk to you when I'm having a week off from everything?"

"If it wasn't for me you wouldn't even have taken this week off."

She opened the door and pulled a face at her brother. "Yes, I would. I'm not completely helpless."

Scott wrapped his arm around her shoulders and gave her a rough hug. He looked back at Cooper and grimaced. "My baby sister. Try not to kill her this week, won't you? I know she'd drive a saint mad."

"Good thing I'm no saint, then."

She had pulled off her shades, and for a second he caught her glance. The ghost of a smile touched her lips as though she was remembering what he'd said to her. Before he got his shit together and smiled back, she'd disappeared inside the cabin.

Chapter Six

Paris hooked her thumbs into the pockets of her jeans and watched Scott as he filled the coffeemaker in the kitchen. She loved her brother, but his timing sucked. All she wanted to do was avoid Cooper for the next five days, but he was standing right behind her as though nothing had happened.

Maybe to him nothing *had* happened. That kind of pissed her off.

"You got anything to eat?" Scott frowned as he opened the fridge and saw the contents. "Fuck me, Cooper. You don't eat this shit as well, do you?"

"We went shopping but had to cut it short," Cooper said. "There was some guy taking too much notice of Paris."

Scott slammed the fridge door shut without taking any of her salad. "Didn't take them long to track you down. Are you sure you haven't told Mom about this place?"

She forgot about Cooper breathing down her neck and

glared at her brother. "Of course I'm sure. If she knew where I was she'd be here already." Then his comment fully penetrated—and it didn't make sense. "What does Mom knowing where I am have to do with the paparazzi?"

For a second Scott didn't answer. Then he glanced behind her at Cooper, and that really irritated her. "Well?" Her voice was sharp. She didn't like where her imagination was taking her.

Scott sighed. "Haven't you ever thought it strange the way the paparazzi always turn up when you have a night out?"

Strange wasn't the word she'd use, but what he was implying was horrible. Her mom knew how much she hated having her every little move scrutinized. She wouldn't believe her own mother was selling her out.

She stalked across the kitchen and leaned against the sink. The more distance she put between her and Cooper the better. Before she could tell her brother what she thought of his accusations, Cooper spoke.

"That's harsh."

Yes, it was harsh. She slung him a grateful glance, and he gave her a faint smile. It wasn't quite enough to show off his dimple, but her stomach dipped regardless.

"It keeps you in the tabloids. She dreads the day when no one wants to splash you across their front page."

Her brother was *crazy*. Except, deep inside, she knew he was right. She was living her mother's dream, and her mom had no intention of waking up any time soon.

If only he hadn't felt the need to share all that in front of Cooper. She'd shared enough personal stuff with him today to last her a lifetime.

"We lost the guy." Cooper leaned against the sink next to her and folded his arms. He wasn't quite touching her, but she still found it hard to breathe properly. "Looked random to me. There's no way he could've known which town we were going to."

She couldn't remember a single time over the last year when she'd gone out for a private evening and hadn't ended up trying to evade at least one paparazzo. At least her tightly guarded secret of having been accepted to Brown wasn't out. Surely if it was her mom leaking stories to the press, that juicy piece of gossip would have slipped out.

Scott appeared to concede that point. "I guess that makes sense. It'd be different if you'd found one of them up the road from here."

"If I found anyone stalking her, I'd soon make sure they backed off."

Scott poured himself a coffee. "I know. There's not many I'd trust with Paris out here in the middle of nowhere."

"Oh, for God's sake." She didn't know whether she wanted to hit her brother or just disappear through the floor. "I'm standing right here."

Scott grinned at her. He was only a couple of years older than her but sometimes he acted like the father she'd never known. "You know I'm right," he said, which at least made her mind up for her. She definitely wanted to hit him. "Cooper's the best bodyguard you've ever had. Admit it."

She had a vivid flashback to the forest. Technically she might not have actually *had* Cooper, but in her experience it came close enough. To her intense mortification her face went hot.

"Your sister's in safe hands."

She rounded on him, but there wasn't a hint of a smile on his face. In fact, he looked kind of grim. Her snarky response died on her tongue. At least she had an answer now. Whatever had happened between them in the forest wasn't going to happen again.

Good. She ignored the ache in her chest because seriously, hooking up with her *bodyguard* was the last thing she wanted. That was the kind of thing her *mom* did. *I sure as hell don't want to get caught up in that kind of mess.*

Except Cooper was nothing like Anson, and what they'd done in the forest didn't even come close to her mom's performance.

I should've just kept my hands off him. No way was she going to touch him again. Especially when he made it so clear he considered it a mistake.

At least that means he won't tell anyone about it. Doesn't it?

"Can't be any worse than the last jerk she had." Scott took a long swallow of his black coffee and she stared at him in disbelief. Surely he hadn't told Cooper the real reason why she'd fired Anson's ass?

"Do I need to know what went down there?" Cooper asked.

She let out a relieved breath. Some things just shouldn't be repeated. "No," she said quickly, before Scott could interfere anymore. "He had no sense of boundaries." Before she could stop herself she waved her hand in a circle to demonstrate what she meant. "I just really needed to get away from it all."

"So you didn't collapse on set?"

Belatedly she remembered the story they'd put out as

a cover for her taking off on such short notice. Luckily the network had played along, since it gave them additional Lola publicity.

"No. It was just something to keep the tabloids happy." And to throw them off her trail.

Cooper frowned. He obviously didn't understand why anyone would want to do that, but then he didn't know what it was like, living under a spotlight all the time.

I don't like not telling him the truth. But she'd signed the nondisclosure as well. If she broke it, the network could break her.

Thank God her final episode was airing next week.

"Since I'm here," Scott said to Cooper, "you can shoot off and get some supplies. Damned if I'm going to eat the crap Paris does."

"Oh, staying are you?" She knew she sounded cranky. She *was* cranky, and she couldn't quite figure out why. It wasn't as though she was desperate for time alone with Cooper. Not after what had happened earlier. It was too embarrassing.

The only problem was she *did* want to be alone with him. It was driving her crazy.

"I'll stay for a while," said her blindly insensitive brother. Although did she really want him to guess what she'd done with his best friend? Since that was a massive *no fucking way* she bit her tongue and gave him a mocking smile instead.

"Sure," Cooper said, in that easy way he had. "What'll it be? Steak and beer?"

L ater that afternoon Paris abandoned her tablet, where she'd been checking her Facebook account, and peered through her bedroom window. After a huge lunch, Cooper had managed to persuade her brother to give him a hand in clearing the back yard. He'd found a surprising variety of tools in the old garden shed, and Scott's horrified protests at getting his hands dirty hadn't cut it with Cooper.

It was amazing how much better the yard looked now that it wasn't a jungle of weeds. She repeated that thought a couple of times as an excuse to keep on peeking out through the window, behind the cover of the drapes. But the truth was the sight of Cooper wearing nothing but boots, jeans, and a battered old cowboy hat was mesmeric. *Is it hot in here or what?*

She took a deep breath. She'd never spied on a guy like this before. Maybe she'd take them out a cold drink. She went to the kitchen and grabbed a beer and a couple of cans from the fridge.

Cooper took the bottle of beer from her with a grin that sent her stomach into a free fall. Scott scowled at the can of soda she offered him. "What the hell?"

"You've had enough," she said, trying not to stare at the way Cooper's muscles rippled as he tipped his head back and swallowed his beer. "You're driving later."

Scott muttered something under his breath, but took the soda. That was one thing she'd say for her brother. He never argued with her when it came to alcohol. She guessed her problems when she was younger had affected him more than he'd admit. "You could invite me to stay over."

She popped the tab on her own soda. "You want to sleep with Cooper tonight? Be my guest." Then she took a quick drink so her brother wouldn't guess where her thoughts had instantly leaped.

Sleeping with Cooper wasn't going to happen.

"I don't share my bed with anyone." Cooper wiped his mouth with the back of his hand and appeared to be avoiding looking her way. "Not even you, Scott."

"When you spend the whole night with someone let me know, and we'll get wasted to celebrate." Scott turned to her. "You're a girl," he said, which was amazingly observant of him. "Would you give a guy a second chance if he loved you and left you as soon as he could?"

She had the crazy urge to giggle. She coughed and mock frowned at Cooper, who looked as though he'd like to break Scott's neck. "Is that what you do, then?"

"No." He ground the word between his teeth.

"Don't give me that bullshit." Scott punched him on the arm. "This is only Paris."

This is only Paris. That kind of annoyed her. "I don't know why you want my opinion. You seem pretty sure you know what girls like. You're such a man whore."

Scott toasted her with his soda. He obviously took her insult as a compliment. "I never leave before morning—and the ladies love it."

She made a gagging sound. "You're disgusting."

"He's always been disgusting," Cooper said. "You've only just noticed?"

"Don't change the subject," Scott said. "We were talking about you and the service you offer."

"I've never had any complaints."

She really didn't mean to, but couldn't help glancing at him. Their gazes clashed.

What would Scott do if she backed up Cooper's claim?

She hastily tore her gaze from him and took a long drink to cool herself down. She had no idea what Scott would do, and it didn't matter because he was never going to find out that she, at least, would give him a five star rating when it came to being *serviced* by Cooper.

"You haven't had any complaints because you don't hang around long enough afterwards to hear any."

"That's not the reason I don't get complaints."

Too right it wasn't. Although, now that she came to think about it, his reaction *afterwards* had kind of sucked. Maybe that's what Scott was getting at. Not that she was going to agree with him.

Or maybe it's only with me that he acted so weird? If she hadn't thrown herself in his arms and practically begged for it, would he even have kissed her?

Had it just been some kind of downgraded pity fuck?

Scott laughed. "When this week's done I'm taking you to *Thirteen*. The chicks there'll blow your fucking mind."

She gritted her teeth. *Thirteen* was a newly opened nightclub in Hollywood that had quickly become the place to be seen. Everyone who wanted to be anyone hung out there hoping to be discovered by... someone. She'd visited the club a couple of times, and every guy who'd hit on her had been more interested in Lola and the business than in getting to know Paris O'Connell.

Which wasn't why she was pissed with Scott for suggesting the place to Cooper. It was because Scott had only one thing on his mind when he went to *Thirteen*, and it wasn't dancing.

Cooper grunted in a non-committal kind of way. "I don't

need to go to clubs for that."

Right, and what exactly did he mean by that? She finished off her soda. It didn't matter what he meant. It was none of her business. *As long as he isn't thinking about what'd happened in the forest earlier.*

Of course he wasn't. He *wouldn't*.

"You haven't seen the girls that go there, Coop. I'm telling you, it's un-fucking-real."

She couldn't stop herself. "Yeah, if you like plastic boobs and Botox."

Cooper's dimple flashed as though he found her comment hilarious. She wasn't sure whether to grin back at him or not, but before she could make up her mind Scott pulled a length of her hair. She wished he wouldn't. It made her feel about ten years old.

"You won that fight. Even Mom wouldn't have the balls to bring that up again."

"What fight?" Cooper's dimple was still very much in evidence. She had the greatest desire to kill her brother, slowly and agonizingly, but unfortunately that would have to wait.

"It was nothing," she began.

"The dipshits at *Sunset Heights* wanted her to get a boob job."

She let out a furious hiss. "Scott!"

"A boob job?" Cooper's glance slid to her chest, and she had a hard time not folding her arms and hiding the assets that had caused such a stink eighteen months ago. "What the hell for?"

Okay, as responses went that wasn't so bad. Except now he appeared unable to tear his gaze from her boobs. She resisted the overwhelming urge to squirm.

"They wanted...more." Scott used his hands to cup an invisible pair of D-cups and then froze mid-gesture as he remembered just who he was talking about. "Uh, Paris told them to go fuck themselves."

"Can we stop talking about this now?" She glared at her brother, who at least had the grace to look uncomfortable. If not for the fact he'd backed her up in the face of her mom's suggestion that she at least *think about it for the sake of her career,* she would happily have given him a black eye.

"Too damn right." Cooper was no longer staring at her chest. He wasn't laughing, either. "You don't need to change a thing about your body."

She gave a strangled sound and hoped she wasn't going red. While it was thrilling to know he thought that, it was mortifying that her brother was standing right next to him.

"Change the subject, man." Scott scowled at Cooper. "That's my sister."

"Yeah, and I wouldn't want my sister getting a boob job just because of some sleazy producer."

Paris was hunching her shoulders in an effort to make her chest disappear. She gingerly straightened her spine and pretended to take another sip of her soda.

"All right then." Scott cast her a glance that told her he knew he'd crossed the line, but had no intention of apologizing for it. Just wait till she got him alone, though. He turned back to Cooper. "Next week, you and me — *Thirteen.*"

Chapter Seven

A couple of hours later Cooper watched Scott roar off on his bike. Paris let out a sigh and pushed the front door shut. She'd avoided looking at him since the boob job conversation, and he was still pissed that anyone thought she needed to make her tits bigger in any case.

She disappeared into the kitchen. He had no idea whether he should follow her and reassure her there was no way he was going to repeat what happened that morning, or just ignore the whole thing.

He'd ignore it. Much easier.

"Want a coffee?" she asked from the kitchen.

"Sure." He pushed all thoughts of getting naked with her from his mind. *Yeah*, *right*. Ignoring the memory was going to be *so* easy.

Inhaling deeply, he went in the kitchen.

"The yard's looking good." She pushed a couple of mugs around the table with her finger. "I don't think Scott expected to work his ass off today."

"Serves him right for turning up like that." And for ramming home the fact that Paris was untouchable.

"Let's hope he gets blisters." She shot him a quick smile, and his good intentions withered. Fuck. This was crazy. Everything she did turned him on. He watched her pour the coffee and she even managed to make *that* look sexy as hell.

He grunted his thanks and took a mouthful that nearly scalded the shit out of him. Then they stood in silence for a few moments, until he couldn't stand it anymore.

"I'm going to take a shower," he said, and escaped.

It was only when he stood in the middle of the bathroom with a towel wrapped round his waist that he remembered he hadn't brought any clean clothes in with him. He eyed the jeans he'd tossed off earlier, but they were disgusting.

Great. At least it wasn't far to his room.

He pulled open the door and came face-to-face with Paris.

She raked her gaze over him as if she'd never seen a guy wearing only a towel before. It didn't help that the towel barely covered his junk, or that her gaze snagged on his groin as if she could see what was going on between his legs.

Fuck. She couldn't, could she? Heat rolled through him. This hallway was too fucking small for the both of them. He offered her what he hoped was a brotherly grin and stepped out of her way.

"Uh," she said, as she stepped sideways at the exact same time he did. They ended up practically toe-to-toe.

"Sorry." Her voice was breathless, but she didn't attempt to move again. Nor did he.

"It's okay." He had no idea what was okay, or why she'd felt the need to say sorry in the first place. Probably because he was having trouble thinking of anything but how much he wanted to plunge his fingers through her hair and kiss her fucking senseless.

Back the hell off, Cooper. He'd crossed the line once. He wouldn't again.

"Crappy plumbing, huh."

"What?" Plumbing? What the hell?

"Runs hot and cold." She took a deep breath and he zeroed in on her breasts. Not that he could see much, but what he could see looked great. He swallowed and dragged his attention back to her face. Her lips were parted and her cheeks were pink.

His dick stood to attention and he grabbed his towel before the damn thing dropped to the floor. *She's my best friend's little sister.* He was supposed to be keeping her safe, not thinking of how she looked when she came.

He tried to focus on their conversation if you could call it that. "Yeah. Fucking awful." Truth was he'd hardly noticed since he'd had a cold shower in any case. *Not that it worked.* He still damn well wanted her.

"Better put it on my to-do list." Her voice was breathy.

He cleared his throat. He'd never had a to-do list in his life, but right now he did, and Paris was the only thing on it.

Stop thinking about her like that.

"I can take a look at it in the morning if you want."

She licked her lips. He told himself he didn't notice. "You're kind of handy to have around, aren't you?"

No one had ever told him that before. "I like fixing things."

Her gaze slid from his face to his chest. "You fixed my bike once."

Her *bike*? His fist tightened around the towel as he tried to make sense of her comment. "Oh, yeah." He gave a pained laughed. Shit, that hurt. "Couldn't leave you crying in the gutter, could I?"

She looked up at him again. Her eyes were all big and dark, and her lips were going to haunt his dreams.

"I used to pretend you were my other brother."

Well, fuck. That told him. "You were always the little sister I never had." But that was when they were kids. They weren't kids now, and he sure as hell didn't look on her as his sister anymore.

She let out a ragged breath that sent shivers across his chest. He was going to have to get away from her, while he could still think straight.

And then she ran the tip of her finger over his pecs.

Don't do that.

Don't fucking stop.

Jesus, I'm losing my mind.

"Cooper." Her whisper killed whatever was left of his good sense, and with a growl he dug his fingers into her hair and pulled her toward him.

She tasted just as good as before, sweet and sexy all rolled into one, and when she wound her arms around his neck he forgot about hanging onto the towel and gripped her ass instead.

When he came up for air she looked up at him, her hair all messy around her face. "I don't think of you as my brother anymore," she said.

"Fucking good thing."

Let the fuck go of her.

His grip tightened. "This is crazy. You know that, right?"

"Yes." She pressed herself against him. His towel unwrapped. "God, Cooper. I want you so much."

She was Scott's sister. He would kill him if he found out about this. It seemed a fair exchange.

He hoisted her into his arms, and with a giggle that damn near blew his mind she wrapped her legs around his waist. In two strides he was outside his bedroom. She gasped against his ear as he went in the room and kicked the door shut behind him.

"You sure about this?" If they went much further he wasn't sure he'd be able to stop.

So stop right now. Put her down and walk the fuck away.

Her legs tightened around him. "No." She panted in his face and her fingers tangled in his hair. "But I've always wanted to have spontaneous sex."

He laughed. "You've never had spontaneous sex before?" He carried her to his bed but couldn't let her go. "That's sad, babe."

"I know. Tonight I'll be Lola. How about that?"

"I don't fucking want Lola."

Her smile damn near made him go dizzy. "That's the nicest thing anyone's ever said to me."

"You must meet some weird fucks." He wasn't sure whether she was joking or not, but he had the strange feeling she was serious. "I don't even watch your soap."

She sighed and gave a delicate shiver that caused his cock to throb. "That's the second nicest thing anyone's ever said to me. You're a terrible flirt, Cooper."

He had the insane urge to laugh again. Sex was never something he'd taken seriously in his life, but neither had it ever been this much fun—and they hadn't even screwed yet.

This is wrong.

Except it didn't feel wrong. It felt so damn right.

As he lowered her onto the bed, her hair tumbled over the pillows. She was still smiling up at him, and then her gaze slid south as she took in the rest of his body.

Her smile froze as she stared at his junk. *Never had that reaction before.* Girls tended to like what they saw there. A lot.

He glanced down, just to make sure everything was in working order. Too fucking right it was. With a groan he straddled her, pressing her thighs together. She was still having trouble dragging her gaze from between his legs. Must be something there she liked, then.

"It's your turn." He flattened her palms on the pillows and threaded his fingers through hers. She stared up at him and it was obvious she had no idea what he was talking about. "Say something nice about me."

Huh. Why had he said that? She wanted to sleep with him. That was more than enough—but after all her giggles and breathy little teasing now there was something off about her reaction, and he wanted to know why.

So why hadn't he just asked her that straight out?

The tip of her tongue peeked between her lips. Was she *nervous*? That was such a smack in the face he pulled up, giving her more space to breathe. He steeled his nerves for her to tell him she'd changed her mind.

"Um," she said, and there was a definite waver in her voice. "You have a very impressive penis."

It took him a whole second to realize his mouth had dropped open. "What?" Had she just told him he had a nice *penis*? He'd not heard that word since he'd been in school.

"Yes." Her fingers twitched around his. "I mean I knew it was big from this morning, but I guess your jeans kind of… contained things."

"Glad you approve." He grinned down at her and his impressive penis basked in her approval. He pulled one hand free and started to unbutton her shirt.

She trailed a finger over his shoulder and then circled his nipple. Would she care if he just ripped her shirt open and to hell with the buttons?

"The thing is…it's been a while for me."

He grunted in approval as her sexy as hell bra came into view. It was pink and lacy and pushed her tits up like a fucking banquet. "Been a while for me, too." Almost three weeks. A lifetime.

"I'm not talking about a few months." He had no idea why she felt the need to talk at all, but forced himself to glance up at her so she knew he was listening. Kind of. "It's been a couple of years. So that's why I'm just a little…you know…out of practice."

That got his attention, even if he couldn't believe his ears. "Two years?"

"Yeah, well. Hudson was such a jerk."

He fisted his hand on the bed and loomed over her. "No sex for two years?"

She blinked up at him. "I don't suppose you count this morning?"

He did count this morning, but not in the way she meant. "Christ, Paris. Aren't there any *men* in Hollywood?"

"Not like you." She cupped his jaw. It was…odd. But it felt good. "And I'm not just saying that to be *nice*. Are we done with the compliments now?"

Two years. He couldn't wrap his brain around it. Paris was gorgeous, so obviously it was her decision, not through lack of choice… And she'd chosen him.

It didn't make any kind of sense, but he wasn't about to call her on it.

"No." He cradled her breast. She wasn't that big, but she filled his palm. "Your tits are perfect. All right?"

She wriggled, pressing herself more firmly into his hand. "Connoisseur of tits, are you?'

"I know what I like." He pulled back the edge of her bra, exposing her nipple. "I'm going to have to get you naked. This is killing me."

Her hand dropped from his face, and she tugged at the zipper of her jeans. "God, Cooper. Please tell me you have condoms."

"I have condoms." He never traveled without packing a few. Not that he'd planned on using them with her, which was why he'd been caught unprepared that morning. He hooked his fingers into the waistband of her jeans and ripped them down her legs. She kicked them off, and he stared, transfixed, at the tiny scrap of pink lace that covered her sex. "A whole box."

She gave a shaky sigh and scraped her nails along his biceps. "Hoping to get lucky this week, were you?"

He sucked her nipple until she writhed beneath him. Her sexy little gasps made it hard to think straight. He lifted his head just enough so her nipple popped out of his mouth. "Not this lucky."

She arched her back. "I need you inside me."

Who was he to argue with that? He gave her a rough kiss, pushing his tongue inside her mouth until her whole body shuddered. "Hold that thought," he growled, before rolling off the bed and grabbing his backpack.

Pocket. Box. Fucking cellophane. His cock was going to blow at this rate, a situation not helped by Paris trailing her finger across her stomach. Any other time he'd be happy to watch the show but right now he was too close to the edge.

He kneeled at the end of the bed and ripped off her skimpy thong. She was smooth as silk. Not a hair in sight. A strangled groan grazed his throat. A part of him had known that from this morning, but he'd been more focused on getting her off.

"You're beautiful." He couldn't tear his gaze from her. She pressed her thighs together, raised her head, and peered at him. There was a cute frown on her face as though she wasn't sure about his reaction. He shoved his knee between her ankles and forced her legs apart. "Don't hide from me. Let me see you."

"You're staring." She covered herself with her hand. Her sudden attack of modesty was a gut-punching reminder she hadn't done anything like this for years. He wasn't sure why that was such a turn-on, but hell, it turned him inside out. He crawled further up the bed, pushing her legs wider, until he loomed over her.

"I'm not staring. I'm drinking in the sight of you naked in my bed."

She pulled her hand from between her legs, and it brushed against his dick. He swallowed a groan.

"You say the best things." She hooked her ankles around

his calves and his cock nudged her stomach. "I don't care how many times you've said them before."

He braced his weight on his elbows and cupped her breasts, pushing them together until they all but spilled from her sexy bra. "I've never said that before."

"So nice," she gasped. "You not being an actor. Means I can believe you."

She scraped her nails along his back and dug them into his ass. He pushed his hand between their bodies. She was so wet, and bucked against him when he circled her slick little clit.

"Believe this," he growled and thrust into her. *Christ.* The sound of her shocked gasp mingled with the roar in his head. She was so fucking tight he forgot how to breathe.

"Jesus, Cooper." Her panted words and the way she gripped his ass shoved him further to the edge. "Fuck. Oh my God."

He pulled out a fraction. She squeezed his length so damn hard he thought his balls would explode. His brain was fried but he managed two words. "You okay?"

She bucked, and he slid fully inside her again. He gritted his teeth and tried to hang on, but her flushed face and glazed eyes were doing crazy things to his self-control.

"You're like a fucking caveman." She was panting so hard he could barely understand her. "I can't move."

He huffed out a laugh and Paris shuddered all around him. Pressure built, and he flexed his hips. Slow at first, but that didn't last long.

Neither would he.

Especially when Paris started to move. He closed his eyes but it didn't help, so he opened them and watched her face—the wrong thing to do. Her face was…glowing.

Hell, he was losing it. He gritted his teeth. She arched into him, squeezing his cock like nothing he'd experienced before.

He buried his face in her shoulder and came… like a fucking caveman.

Chapter Eight

Cooper stirred, rolled onto his side and, still half asleep, reached for Paris.

The bed was empty. He cracked open one eye, and the hallway light coming through the gap at the bottom of the door confirmed it. She wasn't there.

He rolled onto his back and dropped his arm across his eyes. When the hell had she snuck out of his room? They'd fallen asleep together. He'd woken her in the early hours and she'd been all over him. And then everything was blank.

He exhaled a long breath. His dick was rock hard but he refused to grip it for some early morning relief. While it was nothing unusual to wake up with a hard-on, this time it was because he'd been dreaming about Paris.

And he'd expected her to be here. In his bed. So they could fool around again.

Before he could stop himself he wrapped his hand around his cock. He and Paris had done a lot more than *fool around.* He'd slept with Scott's little sister.

He wanted to sleep with her again.

With a grunt of self-disgust he wrenched his hand away. A few more moments slid by, and then it hit him why he was feeling so pissed.

She'd waited until he was asleep before she'd left. Why had she done that?

It took a few more moments before the answer slithered through his sleep-deprived brain.

She hadn't wanted to spend the whole night with him.

He didn't know why that bugged him. He never spent the whole night with a girl. It was kind of disturbing to realize he hadn't thought any further than getting inside her when he'd carried Paris in here last night.

He frowned and tried to get comfortable. It wasn't happening. He reached for his cell and squinted at the time.

Almost five.

Not worth trying to get back to sleep. He'd check out that episode Paris had told him about. He went online and searched for "*Sunset Heights porn episode*."

The internet connection was slow as hell but finally about ten thousand hits came up. He picked the first half-legit looking one.

"Huh." Why hadn't she told him—

The bedroom door slowly opened and she inched into the room, as though she were in a spy movie. She stopped dead when she saw him sitting up in bed.

"I'm sorry." He had no idea why she was whispering, but who the hell cared. She'd come back. "I didn't mean to wake you. I needed the, um, bathroom."

Of course she had. Why hadn't he thought of that? It

was the most obvious reason why she'd left.

She was wearing a pair of boxers and a tight sleeveless top. Forget about the bathroom. Had she left the room just so she could get some pj's?

It was kind of funny. He wasn't sure she'd appreciate it if he laughed. Maybe that's what all girls did in the early hours. How would he know?

"You didn't, babe. Come back to bed." He pulled back the sheet, and she hopped back in and snuggled up to him. She smelled gorgeous, like she'd just had a shower, except she wasn't damp. And was that minty undertone toothpaste?

Had she just brushed her teeth?

He bent his head and looked at her from the light of his cell. Her hair looked perfect. All smooth and bouncy. Not like she'd spent half the night with it wrapped around his fist.

"What?" She pulled back from him and raked her fingers through her hair. "Something wrong?"

"No." There was nothing wrong, but something wasn't quite right. He couldn't nail it down, though. He tugged her back to his side, and was about to throw his cell onto the nightstand and get down to business when he caught sight of the page he'd been reading. "Hey, you didn't tell me you'd won an award."

She glanced at his cell. "You didn't ask. Anyway, I guess I thought you already knew."

He never read the tabloids that Ella loved so much. How would he know Paris had won the Viewers Award for Most Popular Actress for her performance in the Christmas episodes of *Sunset Heights*?

"You'll be up for the Oscars next."

"Huh. I need to be in movies for that."

He remembered something she'd told him yesterday. "That's next on your list, right?"

She didn't answer right away. Then she wriggled against him and wrapped her arm around his waist. "Maybe."

"That'd make my gran's day. She's always said you should get into movies."

Paris sat up and stared at him. "Your gran said that?" She sounded amazed. "She's still going then?"

He laughed and pulled her back into his arms. "Yeah, and don't let her hear you say anything like that. She's still handy with a frying pan."

"She used to scare the crap out of me."

He wound her hair around his fingers and rubbed his jaw across the top of her head. He'd never had a conversation with a girl in his bed at five in the morning before. Definitely never when he had a hard-on. Despite that discomfort, this was kind of nice.

"You know that's all a front. She's a kitten."

"Hmm." Paris didn't sound convinced. "You're just biased. Even kittens have sharp claws."

"Aw, babe. Did she ever scratch you?" He tugged on her hair. She slapped his stomach.

"No. I don't think she ever even noticed me."

"Sure she did. Why'd you think she's so hooked on your soap? She tells everyone who'll listen how you used to hang out in her kitchen as a kid."

"Oh, God." She buried her face against his chest. "I'm surprised she hasn't been cornered by the paparazzi."

"She was a few years ago." He snorted as he remembered how his gran had dealt with the poor bastard. "Guy sued her for assault. We're talking about a thirty-year-old in prime condition being flattened by a little old lady. Me and my brothers had a quiet word with him. He was happy to drop all charges."

She looked up at him. "Your gran flattened him?" She sounded as though she didn't know whether to believe him or not.

"Sure she did. With the help of a toaster. No one ever bothered her again."

Paris giggled and drew circles on his chest. "You're so full of it."

"It's true. I just pointed out to the guy how it'd look for his career if it got out that a seventy-year-old on a disability pension had almost knocked him out. He reconsidered his options."

"I bet he did." Paris pressed a kiss to his nipple, and then gave it a gentle suck. He tangled his fingers in her hair and kept her there.

"Why did you put clothes on?" He slipped his hand into her boxers and palmed her butt.

"Didn't feel right, wandering around naked." She licked him and then pulled back to frown up at him. "Is this the first time you've spent the whole night with a girl?"

"Don't believe everything your brother tells you." Shit. Why had he brought Scott into it? He was the last person he wanted to think about when he was in bed with Paris. He hoped she wasn't going to freak out.

"Don't evade the question." She gave his nipple a tweak.

"Hey, watch it. Don't damage the goods." He squeezed her butt and she squealed in mock outrage. He grinned at her. What did it matter if he told her the truth? "And yeah, this is the first time I've spent the whole night with a girl. It wasn't so bad after all."

"Sweet-talker." She shimmied until she was straddling him. The soft cotton of her boxers brushed his thighs as she angled herself over the length of his dick. "It wasn't bad at *all*."

He tugged at her boxers. They were cute, but her bare ass was better. "What about you? Is this the first time you've spent all night with a guy?"

It might've been, for all he knew.

She wobbled as she pulled off her boxers and tossed them aside. "I slept with Hudson six times. So last night wasn't my first time." She leered at him, and he laughed.

Until her words actually penetrated his brain.

She'd mentioned Hudson yesterday. In fact, Hudson was the reason she'd gone for two years without sex.

It had to be the same guy Scott had told him about. The one who'd broken her heart. How else would she remember how many times she'd slept with the bastard?

"Six times?" Shit, he hadn't meant to say that out loud. "How long were you with him, half a week?" He hadn't meant to voice that thought, either.

"Three months." Paris sat back on his thighs and pulled her top over her head. He forgot about Hudson-the-bastard and cupped her breasts. She fit him so perfectly. She threw back her hair like she was in a shampoo commercial and ran her hands along his arms. "We dated for two months before we did it. Was kind of a let down in the end, actually."

He didn't want to talk about her ex, and he definitely didn't want to think about her having sex with some other guy, but the way she said it…

No way. She hadn't meant what it sounded like she meant. He wasn't going to ask.

"You've had sex more than six times, right?"

She dug her nails into his biceps. "Well, duh," she said. "Of course I have. Eight times now, and if you can shut up for five minutes I'm looking at number nine here."

He wasn't sure why her revelation shocked him, except it'd never occurred to him she'd been so— What was the word he was looking for?

He didn't know. He just knew he was only the second guy she'd ever had sex with.

"Hello, *Cooooper*?" She dragged out his name and waggled her fingers in front of his face. "Still with me?"

He grinned at her. It felt good knowing she'd only had one other guy in her bed. "Looks like it." He slid his hands along her body and gripped her hips, pushing her downwards. "What do you think?"

She arched her back, thrusting out her tits, and resisted his attempt to rub her clit along the length of his erection.

"I think I want to try something different."

He was always up for something different. "Like what?" He hoped she didn't take too long about it. He wanted to be inside her again. Just thinking about how good that felt caused his cock to thicken even more.

She licked her lips and wriggled down his thighs. "I've never given head," she said, and stared at him as though she expected him to do something about it.

He cleared his throat and fought the urge to grab her head and push her between his legs. He fisted his hands and dug them into the mattress before the sight of her parted lips made him forget she wasn't nearly as experienced as he'd always assumed.

"Don't let me stop you." He sounded hoarse. He was

amazed he could speak at all. Never in his wildest fantasies had Paris ever said anything like that to him.

No. She'd just gone down on him without a second's hesitation.

Paris didn't go down on him. She just looked. And then she bit her lip.

Christ, that was hot. He dug his fingers further into the mattress, his muscles screaming with the effort of not touching her.

Then she trailed the tip of her finger along the underside of his cock and he let out a strangled groan.

She snatched her finger back. "Did that hurt?"

He choked back a laugh. "Not in the way you think. You're killing me here. Don't stop."

Her smile damn near took his breath away. Combined with her big green eyes and the way her hair tumbled over her shoulders, she was kind of unreal, like an artist had arranged her so she looked like a painting. She definitely didn't look as though they'd spent a sweaty night together.

"There's just one thing." Her voice was a breathy whisper as she continued to trace her finger over him. He tried to concentrate on what she was saying. It was the hardest thing he'd ever done in his life. "I don't see how anyone could do a deep throat on you. At least, not without suffocating."

He closed his eyes and gritted his teeth. It didn't help the visions pounding through his mind. No way was he going to argue with her. He had the feeling all she'd need to do was lick him and he'd blow.

"Just do whatever you want. It'll be" — *fucking insane* — "great."

She wrapped her hand around the base of his cock and

licked her lips. She looked as though she was about to feast on him. Or at least he hoped. Except, she didn't do anything else.

"Problem?" He ground the word between his teeth.

"I'm just thinking where to start."

Sweat trickled along the back of his neck. He'd already had her twice last night. He shouldn't be so near to losing it just because she was staring at him with awe on her face.

He couldn't stop himself. He grabbed her hand and tightened her grip around him. "Don't think, babe. Just wrap those pretty lips around my dick and suck me into your mouth."

He half expected her to argue. Instead, she braced her weight on one hand, bent over him, and her wet mouth encased his throbbing head. Every instinct urged him to thrust into that sexy mouth of hers, but he managed to pull back. *She's not used to doing this.*

Bright lights flashed in front of his eyes and he forked his fingers through her hair, holding her head.

Her tongue pressed against him. Her head bobbed against his hand. For a second his grip became brutal and then a flash of sanity whipped through him.

He pulled her upward and she blinked her impossibly long lashes at him. *Where the hell are the condoms?* He couldn't drag his gaze away from her to grab one.

With his other hand still wrapped over hers, he pumped himself a couple of times. *Christ, it'd never felt this good before.* She looked down at him and gasped. *Killing him.* It was fucking hot, knowing that she watched.

Can't hold on...

His release was hard and fast, and he collapsed back onto the pillows, still clutching onto her.

Chapter Nine

Paris gasped for breath. She was crushed against Cooper's chest, his hand hard around her head. Not that she wanted him to let her go. God, she could stay there all day doing things to his body.

Watching him come.

Even though he'd pulled her with him as he'd fallen back onto the bed, he hadn't pulled her right on top of his… business. For which she was grateful. She lifted her head. His eyes were shut, and he was breathing heavily through his open mouth.

A satisfied glow spread through her, even though she was still wound up tight inside. He looked absolutely adorable. She ran her fingertip along his nose and he opened his eyes a crack.

"How was I?" She traced the outline of his lips, and his unshaven jaw grazed her fingers. It was slightly weird how she didn't mind talking to him about sex. She'd never been able to talk to Hudson this way. Not that he would've wanted her to. She pushed him out of her mind. It was surprisingly easy.

"Huh?" Cooper sounded drunk. A delicious shudder inched through her.

"How was my first blow job?"

He gave a defeated groan, which made her all warm and wet and needy.

"You're a natural."

She wriggled until the side of his thigh fit between her legs. The pressure against her clit was sweet torture. "You're a pretty good director."

His fingers played in her hair. There was a satisfied smile on his face. "I just pointed you in the right direction."

She rubbed her knuckles over his jaw. "Told you I was a quick learner."

He made a sound of agreement, and then began to frown. "Shit." He pulled his fingers from her hair and started to sit up, still frowning down at himself. She bit her lip to stop herself from giggling, since she was sure he wouldn't appreciate it, and picked up her discarded pj top.

"Here." She waved it at him, and he looked at it as if he had no idea what it was. "It's okay. I've lots of others."

He grunted by way of thanks—at least she thought it was thanks—and took her top. While he cleaned up another thought hit her.

I can't say that to him.

But this was Cooper, and it appeared the filter between her brain and mouth had gone on vacation.

"That's the second time you've come in front of me."

He froze. "What?" There was a wary note in his voice,

and he didn't look at her.

"Am I the first girl you've done that with?" She angled herself across him again, pressing her aching nipples tight against his chest. "I mean, that would be awesome."

He dropped her top onto the floor and wrapped his arm around her. "Not talking about it."

She slid her leg over him and shifted until his thigh pressed against her sensitive clit. How long did it take a guy to be ready for sex again after he'd come? These were things she should know, but she didn't really have a clue.

"Not really fair," she told him. "Seeing as you know *exactly* how many times I've had sex, *and* you're the first to sample my oral technique."

"Feel free to practice your *oral technique* on me anytime."

"I might take you up on that." She'd definitely take him up on that. What would it be like for him to actually come inside her mouth?

The thought of it made her all shivery. Strange how she'd never wanted to try that before, either.

His body shook in a silent laugh. She loved the way he did that. Before she could let him know she wasn't joking, he rolled over, taking her with him, until she was flat on her back.

"Oh, that didn't take long." She wound her arms around his neck. This would make three times in one night. Four times in one day, if you counted their stop off in the forest. Which she did. Was he always this horny?

Then again, until a couple of days ago she'd no idea she was so keen on it either.

"I'm still recovering." His dimple flashed. "But that doesn't mean you're going without."

She threaded her fingers through his hair. "I don't mind waiting. This is nice, with you on top of me." It was more than nice. She loved having his naked body pressing against her, whether they were having sex or not. He was just so lickable and hard and he made her laugh.

"It's very nice." He seemed to think that comment funny, although she couldn't imagine why. "But I'm going to show you *my* oral technique now."

Some of her warm fuzzies faded. "That's okay. You really don't need to." Hudson had gone down on her a couple of times, and it had just been awkward and messy and kind of embarrassing. Especially since he'd considered himself an expert in the art.

When Cooper ignored her subtle hint and started inching down her body, his legs parting hers, she grabbed his hair. "Really, it's fine." She loved him touching her there. But she really didn't want him prodding about with his tongue making her all sore and twitchy.

He looked up from where he'd been trailing hot kisses across her stomach—which she had to admit she liked. But he was getting closer to his target, and she had to distract him without him realizing what she was doing.

"Don't you want me to?"

He didn't sound mad, but he did sound disbelieving. Then again, she guessed most girls loved that kind of thing. She knew Hudson thought she was strange because she didn't come like a firecracker as soon as he stuck his tongue inside her.

"It's not that." She pressed her biceps against her breasts so they went all perky. Cooper glanced at them. Mission accomplished. "I just want you up here so I can kiss you."

She gave his hair another encouraging tug.

He looked up at her face. "Haven't you ever done this before?"

Obviously he wasn't going to give in without an explanation. "Sure." She gave him one of Lola's sultry smiles. He frowned in confusion, which wasn't the reaction she was going for. Maybe she should ditch the act and just tell him the truth. "I don't really feel like it, that's all."

He stroked his fingers over her ribs and along her waist. It was distracting...and wonderful. Goose bumps erupted and liquid heat stirred between her thighs.

"You don't *feel* like it, or you don't *like* it?"

God, why was he making such a big thing out of this? She didn't mind talking about sex with him, but she didn't want to tell him the thought of having a guy put his head between her legs made her want to gag.

"I don't want to talk about it." She gave him another Lola smile. It was the only way she could stop herself from going red and pulling a pillow over her face.

Cooper kept on stroking her, only now he was caressing her boobs as well. It was hard to stay all tensed up when he was slowly driving her out of her mind.

"I'll make you a deal. I'll answer your question, if you promise to tell me the truth about this."

Her question? What was he talking about?

And then she remembered. Now, that was tempting. But was having Cooper possibly tell her she was the first girl he'd come in front of worth the excruciating embarrassment of confessing to him?

Then again, she hadn't won the Viewers Award for nothing. She could tell him it just didn't turn her on. That wasn't a lie, *and* she wouldn't feel like an idiot afterwards.

"Okay. It's a deal."

He eyed her for a moment, as though he was suspicious of her speedy agreement. Or maybe he was having second thoughts.

"All right. In the forest yesterday? That's never happened to me before. I've never gotten in that condition without being able to, uh, finish off properly."

She stared at him, transfixed. Was Cooper Grayson blushing? It was a breathtaking sight. She tugged her fingers from his hair and cradled his face instead. His brow scrunched up in the most adorable way, and she hooked her ankles over his calves in case he was thinking of running.

"Your turn." He growled the words, and her intention to give him a neat and tidy excuse wavered.

Just because she thought what had happened in the forest was awesome didn't mean Cooper felt the same way. Was it possible he wouldn't think she was strange if she told him she thought receiving oral sex was gross?

She took a deep breath. It was one thing to decide to tell him the truth. It was another to actually push the words out of her mouth.

"I don't like it." It came out in an undignified rush. "It's disgusting."

His frown remained in place. It was unnerving. She released his legs and dropped her hands to his chest. His silence was starting to freak her out, but at least he wasn't laughing.

But he wouldn't laugh at her. That's why she'd told him. Although now she wished she hadn't.

Finally he cleared his throat. "You don't like it in theory

or practice?"

Huh?

"It's just nasty." Her face was burning. How had they gotten onto this subject? She should've just let him get on with it and done a Lola. After all, she was very experienced in the art of faking it in front of the camera. Why hadn't she thought of that before?

Instead of backing off, or pressuring her to go for it, he looked fascinated by her confession. That really wasn't her intention. But not only was he not moving away, he kept on stroking her with the tips of his fingers. It was making it hard to remember what she was talking about.

"Is that why you didn't have sex for two years? Because your ex was lousy at oral?"

Oh fuck it. She wriggled, but Cooper just settled himself more comfortably on top of her. She gave up and covered her face with her hands instead.

"No." Well, if she was honest she did think Hudson sucked balls when it came to giving her oral, but that wasn't the reason she'd given up on sex.

Cooper tugged her hands from her face. "Don't do that, babe. I'm just trying to help."

Help? If she weren't burning up with mortification she would've laughed. "You do this kind of thing often?"

"Another first for me." He released her hands and went back to driving her insane with his fingertips. "I don't usually spend much time talking to girls when I'm in bed with them."

She laughed then, although she hadn't meant to. "Should I be insulted or flattered?"

"I don't know. Which are you?"

She ran her hands over his hard biceps. His muscles

were to die for. "I think that's a trick question."

He kissed the tip of her nipple and then slowly sucked it inside his mouth. Her thighs relaxed and she arched into him with a breathy sigh.

"I don't want to do anything you hate." He spoke against her nipple. "But you don't want to miss out on something you might find you like. Not wanting to brag or anything." He looked up at her then, and the evil grin on his face made her so wet she almost told him to do whatever the hell he wanted with her.

"You just did," she panted. "You all think you're so great at it." Had she said that out loud? The look on his face was answer enough. "Sorry. That wasn't really aimed at you."

"Huh. You've got some major issues here, babe."

"No I haven't." If he weren't doing crazy wonderful things to her boobs, his comment would've *really* annoyed her. As it was, she didn't have energy left for anything more than trying not to wrap her legs around him and have hot, unprotected sex.

He kissed her—a long, slow kiss, using his tongue in ways that shouldn't be allowed.

"Your mouth drives me crazy." His husky whisper caused delicate shivers across her naked skin. "I'm getting hard just thinking about you going down on me again."

"God, Cooper." She closed her eyes and gave into the magical sensations spiraling through her body. "Just do me already."

She felt him smile against her throat, before he continued tormenting her with his tongue and teeth. "You want me to stop anytime, just tell me."

Like that was going to happen. She stretched her arms

over her head and writhed beneath his hard body. His mouth was hot and the things he did with his hands were illegal.

He shifted his weight, and for a second she froze, until his mouth landed on the inside of her thigh. Her eyes flew open. Wow. She'd no idea kissing there could be such a turn-on.

"You okay?" His voice was muffled.

"Uh, yes." She snuck a peek of him and then couldn't look away. Seeing Cooper's dark head between her legs was seriously hot.

His hands molded her hips then trailed lower. She wriggled, hoping he got the message, but his fingers didn't go anywhere near where she wanted them. Instead, he touched her everywhere else. Which was awesome, but frustrating. She gripped the iron bedframe behind her.

"Your skin's so soft." He nuzzled her just below where her leg met her hip. For a heart stopping second his head brushed against her swollen clit. "You taste so fucking sweet."

Her legs started to shake. Did he mean her skin tasted sweet or was he talking about something else? *Could* he taste anything else? Did she want him to?

She couldn't stop herself. "What do I taste of?"

He lifted his head and slowly licked his lips as though he was savoring her. It was completely mesmerizing.

"Oranges." He made it sound like the sexiest thing on earth.

She hitched in a shallow breath. "Blossoms. Orange *blossoms*." There was a huge difference. "Is that all you can taste?"

He drew in a long breath and his gorgeous eyelashes hid

his eyes. "Your scent is fucking awesome."

She was so wet. She desperately wanted him inside her, but having his head between her spread thighs was riveting. *Did I really just think that?*

Maybe it was because he didn't make a beeline for her clit, like it was a homing signal or something—and she had to admit, she loved the way he talked while he was down there.

She shifted restlessly. "You got a condom ready?"

"Don't rush me." Now his fingers joined his lips in tormenting her, but he still didn't touch her sex. "Slap me on the head if you want me to stop."

"I'll slap you if you *do* stop." She gripped a handful of his hair and shook him to underline her point. He laughed, a deep rumbling sound that vibrated along the length of her thigh. She groaned and closed her eyes. Every single thing he did felt so right.

His kisses inched closer to ground zero. She couldn't make up her mind whether she wanted him to keep going or not. Her fingers stilled in his hair and her breath stalled in her chest. Was he going to stop? *Do I really want him to stop?*

He brushed a feathery kiss over her sensitive folds. She went rigid, but not because she didn't like it. He followed up with the tip of his tongue. She shuddered and opened her legs wider for him.

Cooper didn't dive in like a cruise missile. He didn't slobber like a rabid dog, or use his thumbs to pull her open like a candy wrapper. He stroked and teased, and the only difference from all the other times he'd played with her was she could feel the heat from his breath.

"You still okay up there?" He followed his question by swirling the tip of his tongue around her clit. She damn near shot off the bed. "Was that good or bad?" He raised his head and offered her a killer smile.

It wasn't bad. Which meant it was… "Good." She tightened her grip on his hair and pushed him back between her legs. She didn't even care that he'd managed to win her over so easily. This was like nothing she'd experienced before. "Don't stop."

He took her at her word. He kissed her as though he was kissing her mouth, his tongue teasing her in ways she'd never even dreamed about. She gasped and writhed and clutched his head. It was too much. *Amazing.*

Her orgasm hit, and a hoarse scream tore from her lips. Cooper kept his tongue on her clit as she came on his mouth.

Never let me go…

Chapter Ten

Cooper leaned on the shovel and turned toward the front door where Paris was madly waving at him. "Breakfast," she called. "Get it while it's hot."

A couple of days ago, the morning after she'd given him the best blow job of his life, he'd shown her how to make pancakes. It wasn't just in the bedroom that she was a quick learner. She'd then made them for breakfast yesterday, and again today while he got on with clearing her front yard.

He strolled into the kitchen to wash. The smell of freshly ground coffee hit him, and an unfamiliar warmth inched through him. He kissed the tip of her nose, which happened to be covered in flour, and then eyed the mess surrounding them.

"This is even worse than yesterday." Sure, she was a quick learner when it came to cooking, but she hadn't yet grasped the idea of clearing up as she went along.

She shrugged. "Cleaning up is boring." She waved her

hand at the table. "I used those blueberries we got the other day, but I'll tell you what, I'm really going to have to hit the gym soon."

He chugged down some coffee. "You're not sitting on your ass all day. Gardening is a good workout."

Paris spread her hands, palms up. "It's killing my hands. Look at them."

He grabbed her hand and planted a kiss over her solitary blister. "I told you to leave the heavy work for me. You can do the weeding."

She pulled a face and pushed him into a chair. "Weeding is boring."

He laughed and dug into his breakfast. She propped her tablet up and started showing him stuff she wanted to do to transform her yard into works of art. He grunted and nodded at appropriate intervals, but his mind wasn't fully focused on pots and paving and fancy arbors.

They had been together for five days. It might've started out as a job, but that had been blown to hell the minute he'd seen her again. The reality was, he and Paris had been living together. Like a couple. And facing that fact wasn't freaking the shit out of him.

He shoveled in another mouthful of pancake and tried to dislodge the thought—but he couldn't. Because the truth was, he liked it.

He liked sleeping with her. Enjoyed waking up next to her every morning. Hell, he even liked the way she spread out all her stuff in the bathroom.

In two days time she was due back in Hollywood. Would she still want to see him once she was back in her real life, surrounded by the glitz and glamour?

He looked at her as she sat beside him. Her hair was pulled up into a ponytail, and she was wearing a cutoff top with denim shorts. She looked like the girl next door. A fucking hot girl next door for sure, but she didn't give off a Hollywood soap star vibe.

But she *was* a Hollywood soap star, and although they hadn't talked about it any more, she'd mentioned she was going into movies.

Even movie stars had lovers.

He finished his coffee and poured them both a second cup while he tried to process what that was supposed to mean. That she would want to keep him as her lover?

Really?

He pushed his plate back and shoved his hand through his hair. What the fuck was he thinking? He'd never fit in her world.

"Hey, are you okay?" Paris ran her hand along his bicep, a frown on her face. Was she concerned about him? Aside from his brothers, the only person he could remember who'd ever given a shit about him was his gran.

Jesus. Get a grip.

"I'm fine."

"It's not my cooking giving you indigestion or something?"

"Nah."

She propped her elbow on the table and cradled her chin. "Maybe I'll cook dinner for us tonight, then. How about that?"

"You're talking meat, right?"

She sighed. "If you insist."

"Sure. I have a cast iron stomach."

"I'm so glad you have so much faith in my culinary

efforts."

He leaned back in the chair and gave her a faint smile. Until this week he'd never shared breakfast with a woman, and no girl had ever offered to cook him dinner.

Truth was, he'd never been in a relationship before, and he was truly fucked up if he thought this week with Paris amounted to anything close to a relationship.

"Bike or car?" They hadn't been shopping since the day they'd come across the guy who'd tailed them. Trouble was, thinking of that reminded him of why he was with her in the first place—as if he needed reminding.

"Bike." Her smile was pure sex. "D'you really think I'd miss a chance to ride with you?"

For one insane moment he almost told her she could ride with him any time she wanted, but the words lodged in his throat. Because what did he mean by them? That he'd go visit her in Beverly Hills once a week? He could just imagine how that'd go down with her usual circle.

Paris was frowning again but before he had the chance to say anything, her cell rang.

She pulled a face. "Oh, God. It's Mom again."

Great. Her mom called or texted at least half a dozen times a day. While a part of him was pissed off by her constant interruptions, there was another part of him that wasn't…exactly. He couldn't figure out how he felt about it, except that no matter what Paris did, her mom was always there for her. Even if she did drive Paris mad half the time.

He let out a long breath and started on his third cup of coffee of the morning.

Paris bit her lip as Cooper drank his coffee. Something wasn't right, but she couldn't figure out what.

Well, that wasn't quite true. She was afraid it was because he was getting sick of her always being around.

She knew from their endless talks, he'd never lived with a girl. Never even had a proper girlfriend, from what she could make out. And yet that week they'd been thrown together like they were an old married couple.

She answered her cell. If she didn't, her mom would only call her again. "Hey."

"Honey, it's been five days. You've made your point. Please tell me where you are."

Five perfect days with Cooper—and she wasn't just thinking of the sex, although that was pretty spectacular.

"Mom, I've told you." About fifty thousand times. "I just need to get my head together. It's only for a week. I'll be back in a couple of days."

She wasn't looking forward to that. In fact, it made her stomach churn, knowing she had only two days left with Cooper.

He appeared oblivious to her conversation. Did he even care she was due to leave in a couple of days? Or could he not wait to get back to civilization?

"Paris, I didn't want to tell you over the phone, but you're on the shortlist for the new *Augustus* movie. It's top secret."

Her mom's excitement made her heart sink. Her mom had wanted her to get into movies for years but Lola was so popular, and once Paris became the face of an exclusive cosmetics brand and launched her own perfume, it was all too lucrative to give up.

Last year, when she'd been offered a place at Brown,

she'd finally gotten the nerve to tell her mom she was tired of playing Lola and wanted to do something different with her life. Her mom had taken it as a sign that the *time was right*. After a fleeting discussion where she said they'd talk about Paris finishing her education "in a year or so", she'd instructed her agent to put out feelers.

She'd gone along with her mom's wish to go for the *Milo Mallory* movie. If she agreed to go for this second one it would never end.

Stop being such a freaking coward.

"Can we talk about that when I get back?"

There was an ominous silence. She refused to fidget, even though those silences of her mom's always grated along her nerves.

"Two more days then." There was a note of finality in her mom's voice. "Okay, honey. I love you."

Paris tossed her cell onto the table. She knew her mom loved her, and that was why she felt so guilty. When she returned home, she was out of time. She had to tell her mom she was taking up her place at Brown next month.

She knew how much her mom loved the Hollywood lifestyle, but it wasn't as though Paris wanted to give up her career forever. Just a few years while she earned her longed for degree.

"Guess your mom's missing you."

She looked at him. There was a brooding expression on his face. What he was thinking?

"Guess so." She wanted to tell him about her acceptance to college and her dilemma about the movies but wasn't sure where to start.

"Had enough of living in the wilds?"

"I could get used to it." She gave him a mocking smile so he wouldn't guess she could get used to practically anything as long as he was there with her. How pathetic was that. It didn't change the way she felt, though.

"At least you have a weekend retreat now."

"True." She glanced out of the window. He'd done a really fabulous job of tidying everything up. There was still a ton of work to do, though. She had no idea what was happening between them, but maybe there was a way they could keep seeing each other without having to make any kind of decision. "I don't suppose you'd be interested in an ongoing, uh, arrangement to knock the yard into shape, would you?"

Her stomach knotted while she waited for his answer. He seemed to be taking an awful long time to think about it.

"Could be." There was a distinct lack of enthusiasm in his voice, and she pulled up Lola to hide behind before he saw how badly she'd taken his response.

It had been a long shot. Why would he want to give up any of his time to help with her yard? Would he be more interested if she mentioned sex would definitely be on offer?

She didn't quite have the nerve to say that, though.

"Hey." He ran his finger along the back of her hand. "Sure I'll help out, but I'm not a pro in this game. It'll take me much longer to get it the way you want it than if you hired the right people."

She blinked at him. He'd seen straight through her Lola face. It was kind of shocking. Or had she lost her touch?

She was pretty sure she hadn't. Which meant her act hadn't fooled him.

Her insides went all gooey. She tried not to let it show on her face. "I'd much rather have you." And wasn't that the truth.

"You plan on being here when I am?" His dimple flashed. She couldn't tell whether he was serious or not.

And that's when it hit her—the urge to confide in him. Whether he was interested in seeing her again after this week finished wasn't even the issue. She could trust him not to tell anyone.

But she still hesitated. It had been such a secret wish for so long it was hard to share, no matter how much she wanted to.

Cooper was no longer smiling.

"Well, look. I know you won't, but please don't repeat this to anyone." Her face was going red. She hoped he didn't take her remark the wrong way. Trouble was, it was hard to confide in anyone when her trust had been broken so many times in the past.

Cooper was nothing like the so-called friends she had as a teen—and he sure as hell was nothing like Hudson.

"You can trust me, babe." There wasn't a hint of irritation in his voice. If anything he sounded concerned.

Some of the tension drained from her. She should've known better than to think he'd take offense to anything she might say.

"I do plan on staying here more often during vacations. I'm, uh, thinking of going to college to get my degree."

He stared at her. For a crazy moment she thought he hadn't even heard her. Was her wish really so ridiculous that everyone would think she'd lost her mind to want to put her Hollywood career on hold?

"Huh," he said finally, which was hardly inspiring. "Didn't see that one coming."

She had the horrible urge to hide under the table. She wished to God she hadn't said anything. "Yeah, well, whatever."

He grabbed her hand again. "I think that's a great idea, babe. But why's it such a secret?"

She eyed him, not sure whether he was serious or not. "Because..." Her voice trailed away. There was the nondisclosure tied to *Sunset Heights*, of course, but that wasn't the reason she'd hugged this secret so tight. It was because, deep inside, she was terrified her mom was right, and putting her career on hold was a huge mistake. "Do you really think it's a great idea?"

"Why wouldn't I? Wish I'd gone to college. Which one are you looking at?"

He seemed really interested, and he wasn't just putting on an act, because Cooper didn't give a crap about sucking up to her for his own ends.

Warmth seeped through her, drowning the demons of doubt. She reached for her tablet. "Here, I'll show you."

Chapter Eleven

Cooper stretched out his legs and hugged Paris closer as they sat on the loveseat watching some crappy late night movie on the TV. She was curled up next to him, her head on his chest. The lights were dimmed, they had microwave popcorn, and soon he'd be taking her to bed again.

She played her fingers over his bare stomach. She'd already half pulled his shirt off him. "So, what do you normally do on a Saturday night?"

"If I'm not working I'm out with the guys."

"Picking up girls?"

Sometimes they picked up girls. Other nights they just got drunk and ended up playing online games. Occasionally, he got together with his brothers, but since they saw each other most days at work, that wasn't at the top of his list.

"I don't party every weekend. What about you?" He seriously couldn't believe the stuff he'd read about her wild parties and hotel wrecking tendencies. Where did the press dig that shit up?

She made little circles on his stomach. "Sometimes I manage to have a night at home. Mostly I'm rocking it at some night club or whatever."

He frowned at the flickering TV screen. "You should've said if you wanted to go out. We could've found a bar or something." It hadn't even crossed his mind. Truth was, he enjoyed just hanging out with her in the cabin, drinking a beer or two and cuddling up after they'd had dinner.

It was different—something he'd never done before with anyone else. And even though this was the fifth night in a row he'd not hit the town, he didn't feel caged or stir crazy.

The complete opposite, in fact.

She wriggled against him. "I didn't say I wanted to go out. I came here so I wouldn't *have* to keep going out."

"You could just say no." He looked down at her. It was crazy that she was burned out on partying at her age. Then again, she'd been doing it for years. So had he, but the difference between them was she hadn't grown up on shitty backstreet parties like him. He guessed it was possible to get sick of champagne and caviar if you had it every week. Not that he knew anything about caviar. Eating fish eggs wasn't something he'd ever put on his bucket list.

"Sounds easy, doesn't it?" She glanced up at him. "My mom's never liked missing out on parties, though. She's always worried we might miss some fabulous opportunity."

"Why can't she go on her own then?"

She gave him a pitying look. "Because I'm the one who gets her through the door."

That was fucked up. He decided to keep that to himself. "You won't be her meal ticket once you start college. She'll have to get used to it then."

For a second she frowned. Maybe he shouldn't have voiced the meal ticket comment but what the hell. She must know what her own mom was like. Scott certainly did.

"I haven't exactly told her about my college plans yet."

She had told him before her mom? He had no idea what to make of that. "Don't you think you should let her know before you start?"

She shrugged and snuggled closer. "She knows I have a place. She just doesn't know I'm going this year. I'm trying to figure out the best way to break the news to her."

"It's not like it's bad news. You just need to tell her."

She let out a long sigh. "It's just hard. She gave up everything to give me my career."

"She gave up a shitty apartment in a crappy neighborhood for a Beverly Hills mansion. Yeah, I see what you mean."

He knew he'd gone too far when she went rigid and then pulled away from him. Would he never learn to think before he opened his big mouth?

"That's hardly fair." Her voice was all ice princess.

"Might not be fair, but it sure as shit is true."

She glared at him. He frowned back. Her mom might take good care of her but he didn't see what great sacrifice she'd made. He still remembered his gran's comment the day the O'Connells had moved from the neighborhood.

Looks like Cora O'Connell's going to get her wish, then. That girl always did want to live in a fairytale.

Finally she let out an annoyed huff. "You can be pretty rude, you know."

"Babe, I wasn't being rude. I don't know the meaning of the word rude." He managed to keep a straight face. He knew if he grinned at her choice of words she'd smack him around the head.

She groaned and flopped back onto him, winding her arm across his chest. He had no idea what had just happened, but he wasn't about to ask her. He just tugged her close and tangled her hair around his fingers.

"You're the only one apart from Scott who's ever said anything against my mom."

"Really?" He found that hard to believe.

"People don't really tell me anything. Work stuff goes through my agent and my mom, and people are nice to me because they think I can help their careers or whatever."

"Bastards." He tightened his hold around her. "You don't need those kind of assholes in your life, babe."

"Hmm." She didn't sound convinced. "Anyway, sorry I jumped down your throat. It was just a shock to hear you say that. The thing is," she hesitated and he could feel her muscles tensing up again. "I've kind of been having those thoughts about her, too, lately."

"Don't beat yourself up over it. You plan on giving up Hollywood for good?" He picked up his half finished beer from the floor and took a reviving swallow.

"No, I don't think so." She swirled the tip of her finger over the bottle as he rested it on his knee. "But in the future I'd like to pick my own projects. I don't want to play an end-less succession of Lolas."

"Sounds fair to me." He watched her doodling on the bottle for a few more moments before it occurred to him she might be giving him a hint. "You want some?" He passed the beer to her.

She snatched her finger away. "No. I don't drink,

remember."

He remembered her saying she didn't drink champagne, but he hadn't thought any more of it, and she hadn't mentioned it again.

"Okay." He took another swallow.

She cleared her throat. "The thing is, I can't drink. I, um, had a bad time with alcohol a while back."

What did she mean by that?

"Did you?" That was lame. "Okay." He realized he was still holding the damn bottle under her nose and practically dropped it onto the floor. "I wouldn't have bought the beer if I'd known."

"That's okay. I've never craved beer. Vodka's my demon."

It was no good. He had to know. "What d'you mean by a bad time?" Had some sleazy asshole spiked her drink and tried something? His mind leaped to Hudson. Was he the one behind it? Was that the reason why he and Paris had split up?

She gave him a searching look. He hugged her and she relaxed a fraction. "I started drinking when Lola took off in the show. Suddenly, everyone wanted me to show up at parties and stuff. Having a vodka before I went out helped me get through the night. But then I needed a couple. And then I'd need another shot halfway through the night."

"How long ago was this?"

"Six years. I managed to hide it for nearly nine months, but by then I was hooked on it."

For someone who hovered around her daughter's head like a fly, Cora O'Connell had sure dropped the ball when Paris had been sixteen. He was pissed with her mom—that was fucking crazy.

"I'll dump the beer first thing in the morning."

"You really don't have to." She stroked the side of his face. It wasn't sexual. It was just…nice. "I just wanted you to know why I don't touch alcohol anymore. I can't even face it without wanting to hurl."

"That blows." *Is this really the time to make lame jokes?*

She gave a half laugh. "Well, yes. There're times when it's real inconvenient."

"You not drinking isn't common knowledge?"

She circled his nipple. He loved the way she did that. Except it was distracting, and while usually he was only too happy to be distracted, this time he wanted an answer.

"No one really cares," she said, sounding as though she didn't care either. "As long as you *look* as though you're drinking, no one's going to ask questions."

"I don't think I like the people you hang out with there."

This time she laughed properly and gave his nipple a pinch. He crushed her hand to his chest so she wouldn't do it again. He had the feeling she needed to talk about this more than he needed to bend her over the loveseat.

"I'd *love* you to meet them." She gave him a wicked smile. "Would you come to a party if I invited you?"

"Sure I would." He couldn't figure out if she was serious about that or not. "And I'd drink soda in front of the lot of them until it was spraying out of my ears."

"Hmm." She sounded thoughtful. "Maybe I should do that."

"If they don't like it they can go fuck themselves."

"Mom said not to draw attention to it. Just kind of go with the flow."

Anger stirred low in his gut. "Your mom encourages you

to drink?" Just so Paris didn't screw up her fucking *image*?

"Oh, God no." She sounded horrified. "She was the one who hauled me off to rehab when she discovered what I was up to, and managed to keep it all under the radar. She'd have a fit if she thought I was drinking again, but she doesn't want anyone getting suspicious and start digging around."

"They won't hear it from me." Then he couldn't help himself. "But so what if anyone does find out? It's nothing to be ashamed of. You should be proud you kicked addiction to the curb."

She blinked. "Wow. I guess that's one way of looking at it."

He twisted around and pushed her flat onto her back. She tugged at his shirt…and then his damn cell went off.

No way was he answering it. He pulled it from his pocket, intending to toss it onto the floor, when he saw the ID.

He sat back up. "It's my gran," he told Paris. "I have to take this."

"Of course." She curled up at the other end of the love-seat, a concerned frown on her face.

"Hey. Everything all right?" He had a sinking feeling something was horribly wrong. Why else would his gran call him at this time of night?

"Of course everything's all right." His gran's crisp voice rang in his ear. She was great with modern technology, but she couldn't grasp the fact she didn't need to shout whenever she used her cell. "I'm having afternoon tea tomorrow and you're coming."

He raked his hand through his hair and tried to make sense of her words. "Afternoon tea?"

"Four o'clock. Don't be late. Your brothers are coming,

too."

"Look, I can't make it. I'm tied up." He glanced across to Paris, and she gave him a goofy grin and pretended to tie a knot in midair. "I'll come and see you next week."

"No. You don't understand, Cooper Grayson. I'm not *asking*."

If there was one person in the world he didn't mind admitting that he loved, it was his gran. But sometimes she forgot the boys she raised after their father died were now grown men. He pulled a face at Paris and hoped she didn't take what he was about to say next the wrong way.

"Sorry, gran. I'm working this weekend."

"If by 'working' you mean you're with a girl, then bring her along, too."

What the hell? He stared at Paris who frowned and mouthed *what's up?*

He'd never taken a girl to his gran's. None of them had. They were all so screwed up none of them had ever had a proper girlfriend before. Although now that he thought about it, last week his middle brother Jackson had been messed up over Scarlett Ashford. Had he sorted that out yet?

"Are you still there, Cooper Grayson?" That was the second time she'd called him by his full name. She only ever did that when she was in battle mode. It was obvious she wasn't going to accept defeat in this one.

"Yeah, but..." He glanced at Paris again. "What makes you think I'm with a girl anyway?" He knew his gran wasn't referring to a casual pick up. She fucking *knew*.

"I don't have time to play your games. Be here at four tomorrow. Jackson has news." And then she hung up.

Well, fuck.

"Trouble?" Paris crawled along the loveseat and strad-dled him. He dropped his cell next to them and wound his arms around her.

"Say no if you want. It's fine. But we've been invited to *afternoon tea* tomorrow." He didn't think she'd want to go. Why would she want to return to the tough L.A. neigh-borhood she left behind ten years ago? But he still felt he should ask her before he called his gran in the morning to let her know he couldn't make it.

She tilted her head and appeared to be thinking about it. He hadn't expected she'd need to think about her answer. No way was she going to say yes. Maybe she was just being polite.

Fuck being polite. Tomorrow was the last day they had together. No way was he going to share her with anyone. Not even his gran. He started to undo the buttons on her shirt.

And then she spoke. "I'd love to go visit your gran tomorrow."

Chapter Twelve

Paris stealthily checked the time on her cell. It was almost four in the morning. She glanced across at Cooper, who was flat on his back in her bed, one muscled arm thrown across his eyes.

From the light of her cell she drank in his gorgeous perfection. The sheet barely covered his goods, and his chiseled abs were a thing of beauty. She dug her nails into the palm of her hand to stop herself from stroking him. The last thing she wanted was for him to wake before she'd freshened up.

Just like she had every morning that week, she slid out of the bed and crept into the bathroom. It didn't matter whether they spent the night in Cooper's room, or her own, this ritual never changed.

She picked up her toothbrush. Today was officially the last full day she could claim his time. She'd told her mom she'd be back home tomorrow and Cooper would be going back to do whatever it was he was scheduled to do.

But last night he'd invited her to go visit his gran.

Her stomach churned. Alice Flanagan might've scared her when she'd been a little girl, but that wasn't the reason she'd not been able to sleep when they'd finally fallen into bed.

It was because *Cooper had asked her to go with him.*

He could've made any number of excuses to his gran. If it came to that, he could've just told Paris they needed to cut the week short. As far as she was concerned, there was only one reason why he'd asked her, and that was because he wanted her to go with him.

She rinsed out her mouth and couldn't stop the ridiculous grin from spreading across her face. It was crazy to be so excited, but she couldn't help herself. It was like a big step forward. This week had been unreal, the way they'd hidden away from the world. But if he was fine about them going back to her old neighborhood where anyone and everyone could see them, then surely that meant he wanted more than just one week together?

She sure as hell did. It was kind of scary just how much she wanted him in her life. Scott could rant as much as he wanted. It wouldn't change anything.

She didn't want to change anything when it came to him, but she wanted to change *everything* when it came to the rest of her life.

As she began to fill the sink with warm water, the door burst open and Cooper strode in. He smacked on the light and for a second she blinked, blinded.

Fuck no. He couldn't see her looking like this. She grabbed a towel and hid behind it.

Cooper hadn't been asleep when Paris slipped out of bed. He'd thought she needed the bathroom—until he heard the water running, and the vague sense of something being *not quite right* that had haunted him for the last few mornings slammed into him.

He pushed open the bathroom door and she looked at him as though she'd just caught him doing something disgusting.

"What're you doing?" Her voice was high pitched as she clutched a towel up to her eyes as though she was trying to disappear behind it. Any other time he would've found that funny, but there was nothing funny about this. What the hell was she doing?

All her shower things were balanced on the narrow edge of the sink. "It's four in the morning," he said, sounding like an idiot because they both knew what the time was. "You're having a shower now?"

Except if she was having a shower why was everything on the sink?

"What? No." She flapped a hand at him until she realized that made her towel gape. "Cooper, why're you in here? You're supposed to be asleep."

He frowned at her. She sounded really upset. He ignored how she backed away, and pulled her into his arms. "Babe, what's wrong? Are you sick?"

"Of course I'm not sick." She was rigid. He rubbed her naked back in what he hoped was a soothing gesture. "I'm just—look, just go back to bed. I'll be there in a minute, okay?"

"I'm not going anywhere until you tell me what's wrong." His gaze drifted to the sink again and her shower gel caught his eye. She had bottles of the designer stuff and that was the scent that turned him on every morning when he woke up. She always smelled fresh and gorgeous as though she'd just left a pricy salon, and her hair was always bouncy.

Right now her hair was a tangled mess—the way her hair *should* look after a night of fantastic fucking.

Her brush was also balancing on the edge of the sink.

He looked back at her. She was biting her lip and glaring at his chest. "Do you do this every morning before I wake up?"

She attempted to shrug out of his arms, but he wasn't having any of that. Finally she let out a huff and wrapped her arms around her waist. "What if I do? You can't tell me you don't like it."

"Yeah, but why do you do it?" He couldn't figure it out. They'd had sex every morning this week. Except for that first time when he'd checked out her infamous *Sunset Heights* episode, he'd been under the delusion she slept in his arms all night, until he woke her up with hot kisses and a rock hard erection.

But she'd already cleaned herself up and climbed back into bed by then. Was that what girls did? He didn't want to admit it to her, but he had no idea. Seeing as his previous experience consisted of casual hookups, he was hardly an expert when it came to this side of things.

But his gut told him something wasn't…right.

She frowned at him as though he'd just asked her something incredibly stupid. Maybe he had.

"So I don't look a horrible mess first thing in the morning." She sounded defensive. "Not to mention morning *breath*."

Embarrassed heat shot through him and he stepped back. "I have morning breath?" Fuck, he'd never thought of that. It appeared there were a lot of things he was clueless about when it came to spending the entire night with a girl.

"What?" She screwed up her face. "Of course you don't. I never said that."

"I think you did."

She hid her face in one hand. Her towel draped, revealing half of her naked body, which was damn hot, but for once he wasn't distracted. "I just didn't want you to see me looking like *this*."

He was still reeling from the whole morning breath idea. But he couldn't see what she was getting so worked up about when it came to how she looked. She always looked great, but she wasn't the high maintenance chick he thought she'd be. She didn't care about getting mud all over her in the yard and although yesterday when she'd broken a nail she'd sworn in a way that had rivaled his gran, five minutes later she'd laughed about it.

"Why don't you want me to see you like this? You look gorgeous. All messed up and fuckable."

Her hand slid down her face. He wasn't sure whether her expression was good or bad. The silence stretched between them. Finally, she frowned.

"All messed up and fuckable?"

While his head might be trying to ignore the way she looked, his body had been thoroughly enjoying the view. "Can't you tell?"

She tugged her fingers through her hair as she eyed his far from disinterested dick, but she was still frowning doubtfully.

"So you don't care what I look like first thing in the morning."

"I'm just happy to see you in the morning. Thought you'd know that by now." When she glanced up at him, he leered at her in the hope it'd make her laugh. She didn't laugh, but at least she stopped frowning.

"Oh." She stopped pulling on her hair and instead hugged her waist again. She didn't seem to notice how the towel had slid down and barely covered her nipples. "I thought that's what you'd want. Hudson said…" Her voice trailed away and she sighed.

A violent burning sensation gripped his chest. He'd never felt anything like it, and it hit him how much he hated the sound of her ex's name. "What did Hudson say?"

She shrugged. "That me looking rumpled with sleep in my eyes wasn't the sexiest thing to wake up to."

"He's a fucking dipshit."

She gave a snort of laughter. "He was very polite about it. Put it down to my inexperience and then said he didn't really mind because he loved me *so much*."

Cooper knew he was glaring. He couldn't stop himself. "You're better off without him." He knew they'd split up two years ago—but Paris hadn't been with anyone else since. Was that because she was still in love with the jerk?

The thought made him sick in his gut. She deserved a lot better than some asshole like that.

"You're telling me." She said it with such enthusiasm he narrowed his eyes at her. "He's a narcissistic prick, and I'm just sorry I didn't see it earlier."

That didn't sound like she was still in love with him. He gripped her wrists and tugged her toward him. Her towel dropped to the floor. "Sounds like you need to forget about every damn thing that came out of his mouth."

"I know." She bit her lip. She wasn't smiling anymore. "I thought I loved him. Maybe I did in a way. Guess it wouldn't have hurt so much if I hadn't cared."

Again that burning sensation speared through his chest. "When you broke up, you mean?"

"Yes. Well, no. It was the way he only stayed with me to use my contacts. Once he had everything he wanted he didn't need me hanging around anymore."

It wasn't often he wanted to punch the shit out of someone. He'd lived his entire childhood under the shadow of his father's short temper and hard fists, and he'd never wanted to follow in that bastard's footsteps.

But right now, if Hudson were to suddenly appear, he wasn't sure he'd hold back.

"Is everyone like that there?"

"No. Apparently I'm just a lousy judge of character. Trouble is, I couldn't trust anyone after that. Were they with me because they really liked me, or because of who I could introduce them to? It's a real passion killer."

He guessed it would be. At least he'd never had that problem. The only thing girls wanted from him was a quick screw.

That had never bothered him before. Why did it bug him now?

She wound her arms around him and rested her cheek against his shoulder. His cock thickened against her stomach, and he buried his face in her hair.

The answer came to him. This was the reason why. He didn't want Paris to only want him for a quick screw. This week had shown him another side of life. One he'd never even thought about before.

Sex had always been available. He'd had more girls than he could count and couldn't even remember all of their names. It'd never occurred to him to want more from a girl, because what more was there?

He closed his eyes and let out a long breath. Everything he wanted was here, in his arms. Sure the sex was fantastic. He couldn't get enough of her, but he liked being with her when they weren't naked, too. She made him laugh, and it was fun having her work by his side, whether they were in the yard or the kitchen.

The truth was, he wanted to protect her from the rest of the world. That's what he did; it was his job. But when it came to her, he wasn't thinking about work at all.

She might be Scott's sister, and the last girl he should've touched, but now he didn't want this week to end. It didn't matter which way he looked at it. Why would a girl like Paris, who could have anyone she wanted, choose him once they were back in the real world?

Maybe he'd see her again after tomorrow, but for all he knew this was their last day together. He'd make sure she never forgot it.

He pulled her with him and turned the shower on.

"A shower? Really?" She looked up at him. "I thought you didn't mind me looking hideous."

He smiled, because she wasn't serious. "I want you wet and slippery up against the tiles."

She gave a little shiver. "When you put it like that, how can I refuse?"

He grabbed her shower gel and stepped under the water. It was cold. He hadn't gotten around to looking at the plumbing yet. "Come on." He pulled her toward him.

She shivered and gasped as the chilly water hit her. Her nipples were erect, just waiting for his mouth. He poured a generous amount of gel onto his hands and smoothed it over her shoulders.

The water warmed up, and the scent of orange blossoms filled the air. He angled her so most of the spray hit his back, and she sighed and stretched as he massaged her taut muscles.

"That's so good." She arched her back, her message clear, and he cupped her tits. She sighed, her eyes closed, and he watched droplets of water slide over her skin.

He squeezed out more gel and massaged her butt. She swayed into him, her slick body sliding against his. He gripped her ass cheeks, and her groan filled his head. Their kiss was slow and sweet, as she ran her hands over his wet back.

She broke their kiss. "Condom."

They were in the bedroom, and he had no intention of going to find one. In any case, the tiles in this shower were cracked and uneven. No way was he shoving her up against them.

"Later." He slid his hand between their wet bodies and circled her clit. She was so silky soft, and her little gasps drove him crazy. Slowly he pushed a finger inside her and her head fell back. For a second he stared at her, transfixed. *You're so gorgeous.* He licked the length of her throat, pressing his open mouth against the frantic beat of her pulse.

Her hand joined his between their bodies, and she grasped his cock. He tried to hang onto his control, but it was sliding away with every glide of her palm.

Her orgasm rolled through her, and her entire body shook. He loved watching her come, the way her eyes fluttered shut and her lips parted. Her wet hair and the way the shower splashed over her face mesmerized him. Her grip on him was brutal and he gritted his teeth, trying to make the moment last.

But he couldn't. With a strangled groan he pumped his release over her slick body and held her tight until the water ran cold yet again.

Chapter Thirteen

Paris watched Cooper from the front door as he did his daily bike maintenance. It was early afternoon and they'd only left her bed about an hour ago. She was pretty sure she wouldn't be able to walk straight for a week—not that she was complaining.

Five minutes ago something had occurred to her. She guessed she should've thought of it before, but she'd been kind of busy.

She smirked as she remembered just how *busy* she'd been, and strolled across the yard toward Cooper.

"Hey, gorgeous," he said as he turned and kissed her, before returning his attention to his bike.

She folded her arms. She loved watching him work on his motorcycle. Or in the yard. Basically, she just loved watching him in whatever he was doing. Mentally she shook herself. *Concentrate.*

"Do I need to pack for a night away? Or are we coming

back here tonight?"

He turned to her. He was wearing his shades so she couldn't see his eyes, but since she thought he was sexy as hell in them, she didn't care.

"Hadn't thought that far. What d'you want to do?"

What she *wanted* was for him to invite her to stay over at his place. It was kind of deflating that he hadn't offered right away. She shoved her disappointment into a corner and pasted on a bright smile. Not quite a Lola smile, since he didn't appear to think much of those, but it wasn't far off.

"I didn't know if you were planning on doing anything after this tea thing. Catching up with your brothers or something?"

He frowned. "You think I'd leave you alone somewhere? I'm responsible for you until tomorrow morning."

She had a hard time keeping her fake smile on her face. *Being responsible for her* wasn't at all how she wanted him to think about her. She tried again.

"Who says you have to leave me anywhere? I could come with you."

He didn't answer right away, and now she wished she could see his eyes. They might give her a clue as to what he was thinking.

"I guess." There was an odd note in his voice that she couldn't figure out. "You could always wear your wig so no one recognized you."

It was like a slap in the face. She hadn't even considered wearing her wig. She didn't even know what that meant. That she didn't care if anyone saw her out with Cooper? Or she actively *wanted* people to see her out with Cooper?

"Sure," she said, as though that had been her intention

all along. "We don't want your gran having to deal with any more paparazzi, do we?"

She hadn't considered that either. All she'd focused on was being in public with him. Why was that?

Because she wanted more than *this* with him.

It was horribly obvious he hadn't given any of it a second thought.

"I wasn't thinking of my gran."

She was starting to wish she'd never come out here and asked the question. She waved her hand in a dismissive gesture. "Whatever." She tried to keep the acid from her voice but wasn't entirely sure she succeeded.

He frowned as though he couldn't work out what her problem was. "You're supposed to be in Europe this week, babe. You don't want your cover story blown, do you?"

She'd totally forgotten she was supposed to be in Europe. The last thing she wanted was for her mom to somehow find out she was only a car drive away. Even though, technically, she was going home tomorrow so none of this even mattered, she still couldn't seem to stop obsessing over it.

"No…" Her voice trailed away.

"You don't have to worry about my brothers saying anything." He took a step toward her, but he didn't reach out and take her hand. "You know that, right?"

"Sure." She hadn't given his brothers a lot of thought, except to wonder if Cooper was going out with them tonight. Which, clearly, he wasn't. She frowned before she could stop herself.

"We don't even have to tell them who you really are. Although, I might have to warn my gran."

Everything he said made perfect sense. So why hadn't

any of it occurred to her?

Because I don't want to hide who I really am with his family.

She hid behind her best Lola facade of couldn't-give-a-shit. "Sounds good to me."

He gave her a weird look, as if her answer sounded off or something. She really didn't want to discuss this anymore. He was being thoughtful, and if she sniped at him she'd just feel mean.

She scraped the gravel with the toe of her sneaker. He still hadn't answered her original question, even though she knew the answer. Maybe she'd make it easy for him.

"Okay, so we're coming back here for the last night, then. It's no biggie. I just wanted to know."

There was a pause. "Yeah." He sounded vaguely confused. She gave him a firm nod so he'd know this line of conversation was well and truly over, and went back inside before she gave him any more reason to think she'd lost her mind.

Cooper parked outside his gran's house, and Paris unwrapped her arms from around him. He couldn't figure out what was going on with her. She was the one who'd wanted them to turn up today, but ever since they'd left her bed she'd been acting really strange. Like she didn't want to go after all.

Before they left he'd even asked her outright. She'd looked at him as if he was mad and then, as she arranged that damn wig, had told him to save any confusion with his family she'd call herself by her third name, Sofia.

He was the one who'd suggested she go undercover, but only because he thought that was what she wanted. He hadn't expected her to try and fool his brothers, but she'd looked so worried when he'd told her she could trust them that it was obvious she didn't fully believe him.

It wasn't that he blamed her for being wary after what she'd told him about Hudson, but it still sucked, because it followed that she didn't want anyone knowing about *them*.

He got off the bike. What the fuck was he thinking? Sure, she wanted to see him again—at her cabin. When she was on vacation, and he could turn up to help out with her yard, but she'd never said anything about them getting together in public.

How could they? Even if she wanted to, Scott would fucking kill him if he found out he'd broken the bro code with his little sister.

He secured his bike and saw Jackson's car was already parked down the street. Paris took off her helmet and fluffed up her bangs. As far as he was concerned she still looked exactly like Paris O'Connell, even with short black hair, but since he doubted either Jackson or Alex had ever watched the soap it wasn't likely they'd have a clue who she was.

He'd already called his gran and asked her to keep quiet about it. No way would she not recognize Paris. She loved *Sunset Heights*.

"Wow." Paris glanced along the street. "Everything seems so much smaller than when I was last here."

"That's because you were a lot smaller then."

She gave him a smile that speared right through his chest. She appeared to have gotten over whatever had pissed her off earlier.

"More than ten years. I can't believe it."

He took her helmet from her. "You've never been back here at all?"

"No. Mom wanted to cut all ties." She looked over to where she used to live. There was a faraway look on her face, as though old memories haunted her. "It's so weird. Now I'm back, it's like I've never been away."

"Nothing much changes around here." And that included his gran. She'd refused to move from this old house when he and his brothers had offered to find her a nice new apartment. Said she liked keeping close to her roots.

"Well." Paris took a deep breath. "Into the lion's den then."

He laughed, and was just about to sling his arm around her shoulders when he remembered where they were. "She's a kitten, remember?"

The door opened and Jackson stood there. "Hey," he said, before looking at Paris.

"My older brother, Jackson." Cooper felt a right idiot telling her that, but she looked as if she'd never seen Jackson before. Then again, she was an award-winning actor. "J, this is Pah, uh—" Fuck, he'd almost called her Paris. Before he could spit out the right name, she gave Jackson a painfully polite smile.

"Hi. I'm Sofia."

"Good to meet you, Sofia." Jackson glared at him as though he couldn't believe Cooper had forgotten her name, before stepping back into the hall and gesturing for them to follow him. He put the helmets under the hall table and went into the front room. His gran was sitting in her usual chair,

Alex was standing by the window, and Ella was perched on the arm of the sofa. He didn't realize Ella would be there, although he should've. His gran looked on her as the grand-daughter she'd never had.

Ella raised her eyebrows at him. He ignored her. From the corner of his eye he saw Scarlett Ashford on the sofa. He'd met her briefly last week, just after his brother hadn't been able to stop talking about her. It looked like they'd fixed their problems.

"So, you're Cooper's girl." His gran had a satisfied look on her face as she stared at Paris. It was bad enough his gran had said that at all, but what was worse was she knew who Paris really was. What the hell was she thinking?

"That's right," Paris agreed. "Nice to meet you."

His gran beamed. She never beamed at anyone. He went hot and hoped his brothers didn't notice their gran behaving like a total fangirl. He turned to Scarlett, who looked as if this was a perfectly normal afternoon for her.

"Hi again," he said. "Finally sorted my brother out, huh?"

Scarlett's smile widened. "You could say that."

Paris nudged him with her elbow. He shot her a desperate look and she just gave him an innocent smile. Innocent his ass.

"This is Sofia," he announced to the room in general.

"Hi, Sofia," Scarlett said. A frown flickered across her face. "Sorry, you just reminded me of someone."

"I get that a lot," Paris said.

"Coop, need a word." Jackson turned and went into the kitchen. Relieved to get out of the heat Cooper followed him. He'd kill for a beer, but his gran refused to have booze in the house. Her gut rot tea would have to do.

Jackson rounded on him. "What the fuck are you playing at?"

He frowned. "Huh?"

"Bringing some random girl to gran's."

That pissed him off. "She's not some random girl. We've known each other for years." Not exactly the truth but not a lie either.

Jackson scoffed. "You didn't even know her name. Couldn't you've taken her home or dropped her off wherever you picked her up last night before you came here?"

"I didn't pick her up last night. Mind your own business, J."

His brother's eyes narrowed. "Is she anything to do with this emergency job you had to do this week?"

Cooper couldn't figure out whether admitting to that would be a good thing or not. "Just drop it, okay."

Jackson gave a disbelieving laugh. "I don't believe it."

"Not asking you to, and before you start, wasn't Scarlett your client at one point?"

"At least I never forgot her name."

He doubted he'd ever forget Paris's name either. "Is that it then?" He didn't want to leave Paris alone in the other room for too long. Not that she'd seemed fazed. No one would guess she'd been nervous of meeting his gran again.

"Guess so," Jackson said. "You know Alex is going to be on your back about it. Pretty sure he only brought Ella along for you."

He exchanged a look with his brother. For some crazy reason Cooper could never understand, Alex always seemed to think he and Ella would be great together. The fact that Ella'd had a crush on Alex for as long as Cooper could remember appeared to have bypassed his oldest brother's notice.

"That's never going to happen." About to return to the front room he paused. "What's this all about anyway? Gran said you had some news."

For a second he could've sworn his brother flinched in embarrassment, but he recovered instantly. "Until last night it was just going to be me and Scarlett here today. Gran wanted to meet her. Weird as fuck. She's never wanted to meet anyone I've seen before."

"You never dated anyone before Scarlett." In the middle of a mocking grin, he suddenly froze, as his brother's words hit him. "When gran called last night she told me to bring along my girl. How the hell did she know I was with anyone?" Let alone anyone he'd actually want to bring with him.

"How the hell do you have a girl in the first place when you can't even remember her name?" Jackson shook his head, clearly giving him up as a lost cause. "And yes I have news." With that, he marched out of the kitchen.

Chapter Fourteen

Paris sat on the sofa beside Scarlett, with Ella perched on the arm next to her. Alex stood in the corner of the room, a watchful look on his face. She'd never had much to do with him. He was six years older than her, and she doubted he'd even known of her existence when she used to live across the street.

Ella was a different matter. Even though she was a couple of years older than Paris, they'd sometimes hung out together in a group, since Ella and Cooper had been great buddies. She'd had a girl crush on her when she was eight years old because Ella was cool and fearless and didn't give a shit about upsetting anyone.

It struck her that she really wanted to talk to Ella, and she couldn't, because Cooper didn't want anyone to know who she really was. And there it was. She felt mean and nasty for thinking that when he was only trying to look out for her—but a part of her couldn't help thinking the secrecy was also because it suited him.

Scott would be pissed if he found out what she and Cooper had been up to, and while she'd gotten to the point where she would happily tell Scott to go fuck himself, she wasn't at all certain Cooper felt the same way.

In fact, she was pretty sure he didn't want to risk losing his oldest and best friend's trust. She couldn't blame him. The truth was she'd never had a good friend like that. The ones she thought she could trust had spilled her secrets to the tabloids. It wasn't the only reason she'd become best friends with *Absolut*, but it sure had been a factor.

Cooper's gran hadn't stopped talking since he and Jackson had left the room. Mainly she was telling Scarlett how pleased she was Jackson had finally found someone. It was all very... She tried to find the right word, but could only come up with *family-ish*.

Surreptitiously she crossed her ankles. She felt like the worst kind of intruder. At least his gran knew who she really was. That had to count for something.

Cooper and his brother came back into the room. He gave her one of his sexy smiles, and she had a hard time not grinning back at him like an idiot. He leaned against the wall by the door and folded his arms.

Jackson, on the other hand, came right over to Scarlett, squashed his big body next to her, and wrapped his arm around her shoulders. Paris shuffled into the corner of the sofa so Scarlett had room to breathe. Ella muffled a snort, as though she found it all highly amusing.

"All right then, Jackson." Cooper's gran nodded at him. Excitement bubbled from her. Had she really once been terrified of this woman? Then again, so far she hadn't yelled while brandishing a frying pan—or a toaster. "Share your news."

She leaned forward so she could see Jackson properly. He was either going to announce he and Scarlett were getting married or that she was pregnant.

"Scarlett and me are engaged. We're getting married at the end of October."

Paris smiled politely. She glanced up at Alex, who was in her line of vision, and for a second he looked sucker punched. She also saw Scarlett's smile twitch. It was a shock to realize Scarlett might not be as confident as she appeared.

She licked her lips. It was hardly her place to speak first, but seriously, *someone* had to say something. "Congratulations," she said. "That's fantastic."

"It's bloody awesome," Ella said. "Well done, J. Are you sure you know what you're getting yourself into, Scarlett?"

That seemed to break the shocked silence, and both Cooper and Alex joined in the conversation. While Cooper laughed and joked and seemed pretty happy about it, she didn't know about Alex. He said the right things, but she got the impression he wasn't entirely *sure* about Scarlett.

Then again, Alex always had been hard to read.

About an hour later she helped Ella and Scarlett clear away the tea things. She'd die for a coffee but hadn't wanted to ask for one when it appeared everyone else was silently suffering through the fragrant tea Cooper's gran poured from a massive china pot.

The cake had been good, though.

Jackson rolled up his sleeves to start washing up, and Cooper had disappeared into the hall so he could fix a picture hook that had come loose. Alex was being all dark and moody in the kitchen doorway.

Did Ella still have a crush on the eldest Grayson brother? It sure didn't look as though the two of them were *together*.

"So how long have you and Cooper been seeing each other?" Ella glanced her way before tossing a tea towel at Alex, who caught it and shot her a half smile before joining his brother at the sink.

"Just for a week." She shrugged, not sure how much detail to give, but when Ella turned and gave her an odd look she gave a little wave of her hand and added, "It's nothing serious."

"Fuck me. I *knew* it." Ella's comment had everyone turning their way. Ella leaned right into her space, and Paris backed up until she hit the stove. "*Sofia* my ass. You've practically trademarked that little flick of the hand. You're Paris O'Connell."

Scarlett gasped. "Really? I *thought* I recognized you."

There was no point trying to deny it. Not that she wanted to, and although Scarlett obviously knew who she was, both Jackson and Alex were frowning at her as if they were trying to place who the hell Paris O'Connell was and why Ella was making such a big deal out of it.

Cooper appeared at the door, hammer in hand. Ella rounded on him. "What're you on, trying to fool us about Paris? Why didn't you just tell me it was Scott's *sister* you were babysitting this week?"

Babysitting? Cooper had told Ella he was *babysitting* this week?

"Uh." He looked as though he'd just been grabbed by the balls, and not in a good way. She didn't feel inclined to help him out, so she smiled at him sweetly instead.

"*This* is Scott's sister?" Jackson stared at her as though she'd suddenly grown a second head. "Little Paris O'Connell?" He glanced at Cooper. She thought she saw a silent message pass between them. What was *that* all about?

"Also known as Lola de la Mare from *Sunset Heights*." Cooper's gran appeared next to Alex. "I only started watching that show because of you."

"Didn't you go for the role in that new Milo Mallory movie?" Ella looked enthralled. "I love her books."

That was the part she'd had a couple of callbacks for. It was a Romeo/Juliet kind of story set in a motorcycle club, except without everyone dying at the end.

"Yeah. It'd be a great role to land." Well, she could hardly tell them her real plans. It was too complicated.

Cooper slid the hammer onto the kitchen counter. Paris didn't look pissed that her disguise had been rumbled. He should've known Ella would put the pieces together. He'd told her he was doing a favor for Scott but hadn't gone into any details, and she'd jumped to the babysitting thing all by herself.

He got the feeling Paris hadn't been too impressed by that comment.

"So Paris is your client this week?" Alex said, so only he could hear. Not hard, since Ella and his gran were bombarding Paris with questions.

He didn't answer right away. He'd never thought of her as his client, and he sure as hell didn't now, but calling her that would certainly stop Alex asking any more probing questions that he wasn't ready or able to answer.

"Yeah." Then he couldn't stop himself. "But not officially. Scott didn't want her off the grid without some protection around." And fine protection he'd turned out to be.

"She's got trouble?" Alex folded his arms and leaned back against the doorframe. He looked completely relaxed, but Cooper wasn't fooled. Paris might've lived like a Hollywood princess for the last ten years, but when it counted she was still one of them—the little girl who'd once lived across the street.

And Alex always looked after his own. Christ, didn't he know it.

"Nothing I can't handle. Just paparazzi, that's all."

Paris was talking about some movie she was involved in where the rich girl slummed it so she could win her bad boy hero. He frowned. He thought she was starting college this fall.

Maybe she just didn't want to share her plans. His tense muscles relaxed. Why would she? She hadn't even told her mom yet.

She really was a great actor. She'd almost fooled him there for a minute.

It was early evening when Jackson and Scarlett left, with Alex and Ella following soon after. Paris excused herself to use the bathroom and Cooper retrieved their helmets from the hall.

His gran loomed beside him, all five foot three of her.

"Are you and her serious?"

"*What*?" His gran had never asked him about his sex life before. He guessed she wasn't actually asking about his sex life now, either, but his guilty conscience went there anyway.

Her lips twitched. "Cooper Grayson, don't you try giving me that innocent look. I've seen you hanging about with plenty of girls over the years."

Fuck. What the hell? She *had*?

"And I've never seen you look at any of them the way you look at her."

He took a step backward and nearly knocked over the hall table. "We're just friends. She's Scott's little sister."

"Scott's got nothing to do with it." She followed him up the hall until his back was flat against the front door. "I heard something in your voice when I called you last night. You sure weren't playing tiddlywinks with her."

Tiddlywinks? What the hell was that?

"Why else d'you think I told you to bring her along?" His gran flashed a triumphant smile. "'Course, I had no idea it was Lola. Now I just need to see your pigheaded big brother settled, and I'll be done."

Paris came down the stairs. He'd never been so relieved to get away from his gran before. Once outside he sucked in great lungs full of air and turned to look at her.

"You hungry?"

She leaned in toward him as they made their way to his bike. "I'd commit murder for a coffee."

Chapter Fifteen

They went to a local steakhouse, and Paris drank two coffees straight down before she leaned back in the booth and let out a long sigh. "That tea your gran served up was foul."

"You're lucky you didn't have to drink the stuff every Sunday afternoon."

She smiled and then ducked her head when the waitress brought over their order. Once they were alone again she picked up her fork and jabbed it in his direction. "I don't think Alex was thrilled about Jackson's news."

How would she know that? Alex hadn't said much about it at all, as far as he could remember. "You think?"

She looked at him. He itched to pull that damn wig off her head. "His body language, Cooper. Didn't you notice?"

Why would he notice something like that? "No."

"He's very—" she paused and scrunched up her face in thought. She looked so cute. He let out a silent sigh and had to admit his gran was right about one thing.

He'd never looked at another girl the way he looked at Paris.

"*Contained*," she said. "He doesn't give much away, but he was pretty much floored by Jackson's news."

Contained summed up Alex well—and then the familiar gnawing of guilt ate through his gut.

Alex hadn't always been so rigidly self-controlled.

"What's the matter?" The concern in her voice pulled him back to the present, and he shook his head.

"Nothing." He wasn't going to talk about the past. It didn't do any good or make any difference. He could only hope Paris didn't remember anything about that night twelve years ago.

It wasn't likely. She'd only been ten.

She dug into her salad. He thought they'd moved on. Then she looked up at him, and he knew they hadn't.

"About that night…" Her voice trailed away, and she bit her lip. She obviously wasn't sure whether it was something he was willing to discuss with her.

He never discussed it with anyone. He frowned at his steak, but Paris didn't say anything else. So of course he had to look at her.

She gave him a faint smile. "You can tell me to back off, but I only know what Scott told me later—and he always liked to…embellish things."

He doubted Scott had *embellished* anything that'd happened that night. There'd been no need.

"What did Scott tell you?" He picked up his soda and took a long swallow. Beer would've been better but hell, he could live without it while he was with her.

He could probably live without another beer forever.

She twirled her fork through her salad and avoided his gaze. "He said if Alex hadn't done anything, you would've ended up in the morgue instead of the ER."

It sounded like the kind of thing Scott would say.

He gave a noncommittal grunt and started on his steak.

"You mean it's true? He wasn't exaggerating?"

He heaved a sigh and caught her gaze. Her gorgeous green eyes were fixed on him with something that looked like horror. Seeing her look so worried for him did something strange and warm to his insides.

"I knew what I was doing." The words were out before he even knew he was going to say anything. "I could never keep my mouth shut around my dad."

"That doesn't mean you deserved what happened." Her voice was hardly above a whisper, but she sounded so furious he forgot all about his steak. "How can you even think that?"

He'd thought about it a lot over the years. Not so much the fact he'd ended up with broken bones and a concussion, but because if he hadn't pushed his dad over the edge then Alex wouldn't have become involved, Social Services wouldn't have poked their noses in, and their dad...

Who the hell knew what would've happened to his dad.

He didn't want to talk about it. He never talked about it, but there was something about Paris that made him want to spill his guts.

He tore his gaze from her and stared at his plate. This guilt was his. No one else needed to hear it—especially not her.

She laid her hand on top of his and slid her thumb

beneath his palm. "Cooper." Her whisper was no longer filled with anger. "None of that's your fault."

He stroked his thumb over her skin. Why did he feel this burning need to tell her? It was like a rock lodged in the center of his chest. Fuck it. How had they started talking about that night in the first place?

"I should've just left him alone in the kitchen." *So much for shutting up*. But the words pounded in his head and spilled into his throat, choking him. "All I wanted was for him to look at me as if I wasn't a piece of shit on his boot. I don't remember my mom—I was only six when she died—but I can't forget that look on *his* face whenever he caught sight of me."

Paris's hand tightened around his, and he dragged his reluctant gaze up to hers. She swallowed and pressed her lips together, her eyes glassy.

She didn't say anything.

Shut the fuck up. But it was as if he'd pulled a scab from a festering wound, and the poison just kept on coming.

"I don't even remember Alex hauling him off me. I was well out of it by then." He fisted his other hand on the table and stared at it. All he could see was Jackson's battered face as he told Cooper the cops had dragged Alex off to juvie.

"It was your dad's fault." The worried look was back on her face. "You do know that, right?"

This was getting way too heavy. He didn't want to spoil whatever it was he had with Paris with the ugly brutality of his childhood. He tried to laugh, to lighten the mood, and turn it all into a joke, but found he couldn't.

"It was my fault, Paris."

When she opened her mouth to disagree, he threaded

his fingers through hers. "Not the beating." He tugged her hand up and grazed her knuckles along his jaw. It felt good. "But what happened to Alex. Juvie changed him, and that *was* my fault."

She didn't say anything. What was there to say? Had he really thought telling her would shift the guilt lodged inside? Because it hadn't. He felt worse.

"No." There was an oddly thoughtful note in her voice. "What happened to Alex wasn't your fault."

She didn't understand. "If he hadn't beaten the crap out of our dad, he wouldn't have been locked up. He's never told J or me what happened while he was inside, but something must've. Because when he came out…" Cooper's voice trailed away. How could he explain how his brother had changed?

She had really summed it up when she'd said Alex was *contained*.

"I'm not saying he should've been locked up. I'm just saying…you're not responsible for what Alex did that night. He made his own choices."

"Because of me."

She frowned and cupped her chin in her free hand. "Yes, because of you. But you didn't make his decisions for him, did you? I mean, you don't have some superpower where you can make people do stuff with your mind, do you?"

If it had been anyone other than Paris who said that to him, he'd have thought they were fucking with him. But he would never have had this conversation with anyone else but her, and he knew she wasn't being sarcastic.

She was serious.

He leaned across the table. "Babe, I ruined his life."

She pulled his hand toward her and pressed his knuckles against her lips. "Yeah, I can see how you ruined his life. He owns his own business, drives a convertible, and wears designer gear."

"That's not—" he cut himself off and frowned as two things hit him between the eyes. One, she had discovered a hell of a lot about Alex during a couple of hours with his gran and Ella, and secondly, her comment struck him as being strangely similar to his when he'd disagreed that her mom had sacrificed so much for Paris's career.

A shudder inched along the back of his neck. He'd never looked at it from that angle before. "Alex would always have made it."

"I'm not saying he wouldn't. I'm just saying you're taking an awful lot of credit for the ways things turned out."

He stared at her. How had she done that? Taken his guilt and managed to turn it into—what exactly?

Pride?

"That's fucking twisted." He wasn't sure whether he was annoyed or not.

She grinned at him. "That's me. Twisted as fuck."

"Huh." For about the hundredth time since they'd left her cabin he squashed the urge to pull that wig off her head. He guessed he wasn't that annoyed with her after all. "So… you definitely due back in Hollywood tomorrow?"

She pressed kisses along his knuckles, without taking her gaze from him. He'd never known his knuckles had so many nerve endings.

Paris hoped Cooper couldn't guess how she leaped to crazy conclusions at his question. He might just be making conversation.

No, he isn't.

"I have a photo shoot at the end of the week, but I don't *have* to go back before then."

He worked his fingers free from her, and picked up his knife. Without looking at her he said, "I've got a couple of local jobs this week. You want to stay at my place for a few days?"

Yes! She'd been right. It was hard not to punch the air. She didn't even pretend to think about her answer. "Sure. Why not?"

He glanced up at her, fork halfway to his mouth. "Yeah?" He sounded slightly shocked that she'd agreed. "Tonight?"

"Of course tonight." She laughed at the look on his face. "I can't wait to see where you live."

Just before they left, he went to the restroom, and as she watched him stroll across the restaurant, more than a few heads turned his way. He didn't seem to notice.

The besotted smile on her face faded. She'd always known that night twelve years ago had been bad, but she'd only been a kid at the time, and Scott's graphic stories had never seemed quite real.

It was a good thing Cooper's dad was dead already, because she wanted to gut the sadistic bastard. When she remembered the haunted expression on Cooper's face as he told her how his dad used to look at him, her chest hurt.

Her mom always used to say the Grayson boys would end up in jail, or worse. She could only guess what her mom meant by *worse*—but whatever. Her mom had been wrong.

They'd turned out fine.

Cooper had turned out way better than fine.

She was in danger of having a ridiculous smile on her face when he returned so she dug into her purse for her cell. Might as well get it over with.

She sent her mom a text, telling her she'd be back by the end of the week and not to worry as she was in their old neighborhood staying with Cooper Grayson.

Then she turned off her cell.

Chapter Sixteen

The following afternoon while Cooper worked, Paris shopped. Not that he realized what she was doing. From what he'd said earlier before he left she got the impression he thought she'd be hiding out in his apartment until he got home.

A squishy warmth stole through her. His apartment was only about a ten minutes' drive from his gran's house but it might've been in a different world. A one bedroom cute conversion in an old 1920s brick building, it had real potential—not that he'd done much with it.

Would he mind if she bought a few things for his apartment? She wanted to do something for him in thanks for all the work he'd done in her yard. God, that had been fun. She'd never done anything like that before. Maybe they could even spend weekends together fixing up the cabin.

This was definitely more than a fling. It wasn't all in her mind. Tonight she'd take the plunge and ask him if he wanted to get serious. As in, officially *dating* serious.

She had a big dreamy smile on her face, and she couldn't seem to hide it. She was getting a few sideway glances as well, but she didn't care. If people wanted to take pics of her on their cells, let them.

She'd left her wig on the bed. She didn't need it anymore, and she didn't need a bodyguard either.

Her cell went off. She checked it and sighed. After turning her cell back on that morning she'd discovered her mom had left half a dozen messages since last night. She had to speak to her sooner or later.

"Hey, Mom."

"You've been with Cooper Grayson since you left here?" Her mom sounded very calm. "Why didn't you just tell me that?"

Paris raised her eyebrows. She'd expected her mom to go bat shit crazy. It was a relief she didn't want a full explanation. "Um, sorry."

"Scott's just told me he asked Cooper to look after you. If I'd known that I wouldn't have worried so much."

Her mom was being very understanding, considering how both she and Scott had misled her. A twinge of guilt ate through her. "I did tell you not to worry." She hoped she didn't sound too defensive.

"Scott tells me Cooper's contract ended this morning, honey. Have you hired him for a few more days then?"

She tightened her grip on her cell. Her mom made it sound like she was hiring Cooper for sex or something. Well, obviously her mom didn't think she was having *sex* with him. If she knew that, she'd be spitting bricks.

Paris didn't know what she and Cooper had together,

but it had nothing to do with business. Now wasn't exactly the best time to tell her mom her plans, but the truth was— there never would be the right time.

"No." She took a deep breath. "I really like Cooper. I want to see how things work out between us."

The silence was ominous. Why hadn't she let the call go to voicemail?

Finally her mom took a deep breath. "Are you sleeping with him?"

Her face heated. No one was taking any notice of her, but she suddenly felt horribly on display. She edged toward a storefront and leaned against the wall. It was better than standing in the middle of the street while her mom asked her about her sex life.

"That's really not any of your—"

"Honey, I know I upset you when you saw me with Anson."

She shuddered. "I don't want to talk about—"

"But it would kill me to know that's the reason why you jumped straight into Cooper Grayson's bed."

Anger sparked through her. "That's not the reason I— That's got nothing to do with it."

"I just don't want you getting hurt, that's all."

"Look, I have to go. I'll call you later." If she didn't end this call she was going to say something she'd regret.

"Scott often goes out with him—and I know the kind of things they get up to. He's not the type to settle for one girl, Paris."

The anger stirred again. "You've no right to say that. You don't know him, Mom."

"I know he likes to drink. I don't blame him for that,

considering the childhood he had, but you need to be careful. You can't be with someone who can't live without alcohol. You need support and someone who understands, honey."

God, her mom had a nerve. Every fucking party and event she attended was flooded with alcohol. Her mom had never given that as a reason why she shouldn't go.

"It so happens he does understand." She hadn't quite realized that until this moment. And while it had only been a couple of days ago that she'd told him, he hadn't touched a beer since. In fact, he'd dumped his stash from the cabin into the garden shed, even though she kept telling him it was fine. "Actually, he doesn't see why I need to keep it all a big secret, either."

"I see." There was a strangled note in her mom's voice. "What else have you told him?"

"I'm not talking about this anymore. I'll call in a few days and let you know when to expect me." With that she hung up. God, she needed a coffee.

It was almost seven before Cooper returned home. Strange, he'd never really thought of it as home before. It was just a place where he crashed, occasionally cooked himself something to eat, and had friends over to watch a game on the big screen. He'd only bought the minimum of furniture and a lot of his crap was still packed in boxes.

But at odd times during the day he'd found himself looking forward to coming back here, just so he could see Paris again.

He'd never really looked too far into the future. He'd been

renting this apartment for a couple of years and it was fine for him. Both his brothers had taken out hellish mortgages to buy their places, and he'd never really understood why.

Now, for the first time, he did.

He let out a long breath. He wanted to ask her to move in with him. Until last night he hadn't even thought *that* far ahead. And now he couldn't think of anything else. Except why would she want to?

But when he'd asked her to stay with him for a few more days, she didn't hesitate. He was still kind of shocked by that. He half expected her to have disappeared first thing that morning, but she'd cooked him pancakes again.

He paused, front door key in hand. It was one thing asking her to stay for a few days. It was another to ask her if she wanted to move in permanently when she was on vacation from college. And while a part of him still couldn't believe she'd want anything longer than a quick fling with him, there was another part of him—a big part—that desperately hoped she did.

Which meant he had to think ahead. His apartment wasn't big enough for two. Hell, he still couldn't believe the amount of stuff she'd taken to the cabin for just a week. He wasn't sure he could imagine how big a closet she'd need for real.

He'd make sure she knew he'd find them somewhere bigger. Fuck the repayments.

The door swung open before he even got the key in the lock. Paris stood there, her gorgeous red-gold hair tumbling over her shoulders in the way he loved and there was a wicked smile on her face.

"Had a good day at the office, dear?" She wrapped

her arms around his neck and gave him a kiss that wiped all thoughts of ball-breaking mortgages from his mind. She pulled him into the apartment, and he kicked the door shut.

"First time anyone's greeted me like that."

"I should hope so." She stepped away, hands on her hips. "Just so long as you're not expecting anything to eat the minute you get home. Even I can see having pancakes more than once a day is kind of excessive."

He wound his arm around her waist and tugged her back. "You taking cooking classes at college, then?"

She smacked his chest. "The hell I am. That's what a housekeeper's for."

"Bit of a princess really, aren't you?"

She squeezed his butt. "You love it."

He laughed as they entered his open plan living area, and then he stopped laughing. "Fuck me."

Paris tensed, but she didn't pull out of his arms. "You don't like it? I didn't mean to…well, I mean it looks like you've only just moved in and not really got sorted. And I just wanted to do something as a thank you for everything, but you don't need to keep any of it if you don't want."

The apartment had stripped timber floors throughout. It'd never occurred to him to do anything else with it. Now a massive rug covered the floor in front of the flat screen, and huge cushions took up half the space on his two mismatched sofas.

He blinked. There were even a couple of small square tables between the sofas, with modern looking lamps on them.

"You've been shopping." It was stating the glaringly obvious, but he had no idea what else *to* say. Whatever he'd thought she had done today, buying stuff for the apartment hadn't come close.

"I do love shopping," she said. "I have a knack for it."

"Good thing one of us has. I hate shopping."

She frowned. "Oh, well, I don't love grocery shopping. In case you were wondering. Takeout okay?"

He had a better idea. He'd never taken a girl out on a proper date before—and while he and Paris had been out together a few times, she'd always worn her wig so in a way it didn't count.

"Give me ten minutes. We'll eat out."

In his bedroom a dozen fancy bags lay scattered across the floor. Obviously she had bought a lot more than just a rug and cushions. Where the hell had she managed to find room for it all?

Since she clearly had, he went through into his compact bathroom and had the quickest shower in his life. He'd just finished pulling on fresh jeans when his cell went.

It was Alex. "Hey."

"Ella's just told me you and Paris are living together." There was no censure in his brother's voice but he heard it all the same. If Jackson had called and said that, Cooper would've given him some smart comment about minding his own business.

But this was Alex, and no matter what Paris said about him not being responsible for his brother's actions in the past, the guilt still ran deep.

There was only a four-year age gap between them, but in a way Alex was the dad Cooper had never had.

"That's right." Shit, did he sound defensive? His muscles tensed. He always went on the defensive when he went up against Alex.

He owed Alex his life. He knew that. Fuck, everybody knew that. Just like everyone knew if not for him, Alex would never have ended up inside.

It was the reason he went along with whatever his brother wanted. Most of the time it suited him. And when it didn't, he only had to remember just how big a debt he owed Alex.

"Ella seems to think it's got nothing to do with you protecting her from the paparazzi."

Ella was right. He raked his fingers through his hair. Alex was going to find out sooner or later. He might as well get it over with. "No. It's personal."

There was a silence. Alex was an expert when it came to serving up a significant silence.

Finally he spoke. "You know nothing's going to come of this, don't you, Coop."

It wasn't even a question. He clenched his jaw and swallowed his burning retort. *Why the fuck not* would tell Alex a whole lot more than he was prepared to share.

A prickling sensation skated along the back of his neck. He swung round and Paris was at the bedroom door, a questioning smile on her face.

Chapter Seventeen

Paris had gone upstairs to find the cute coral jacket she'd bought that afternoon. Cooper was standing in the middle of his bedroom with his back toward her, wearing only his jeans with his cell at his ear, and for a few mouth watering seconds she drank in the perfection of his ripped body. Suddenly going out with him wasn't nearly as important as pinning him to the bed and exploring every gorgeously toned muscle he possessed.

Until he turned around and caught sight of her. The look on his face was like a punch in the stomach. What had happened? Who was he talking to? She frowned, but his gaze slipped from hers, and he made his way to the closet and pulled out a shirt.

Weird. For a second there he'd looked really guilty. She couldn't think why he would look at her and feel guilt. She joined him at the closet where she'd hung her jacket. Good thing she'd bought hangers while she was out today.

Cooper stepped away from her. It was almost as though he thought she was trying to eavesdrop on his conversation.

What was the matter with her? Paranoid much? She shook her head and pulled on her jacket as he muttered something unintelligible into his cell and ended the call.

"Everything okay?" She turned and smiled at him. He smiled back, but for some reason it sent a strange little chill through her.

"Everything's great."

She glanced at the end of the bed, where she'd left her wig. He followed her gaze. There was an awkward silence, although she couldn't figure out why it was uncomfortable. They often snuggled in silence while watching movies on the flat screen.

Then again, they were neither snuggling nor watching movies right now.

He picked up her wig and handed it to her.

Her heart gave a strange lurch as she took it from him. His message could hardly be clearer.

It didn't matter. It was only a small thing. So what if he wasn't ready for anyone to know they were seeing each other?

They *were* seeing each other, right? They were living together.

She fixed the wig and watched Cooper's reflection in the mirror as he buttoned his shirt. The truth jabbed through her, but she tried to ignore it.

We're not living together at all. He'd only invited her to stay for a few days. Her plans of asking him tonight if he wanted to *get serious* faded.

Best wait a couple more days. She didn't want to

scare him off. She might not be an expert when it came to relationships, but compared to him she was a pro.

There was no rush. She could take this nice and slow.

By the time they arrived at *Murphy's*, an Irish pub that apparently served great food, she'd almost managed to convince herself this was the way she'd wanted the night to go.

Almost.

"The restaurant's separate from the main bar," Cooper said as he took the helmet from her. At least she didn't have to worry about helmet hair. The wig would still look good if she'd ridden through the apocalypse. "I thought that'd be okay?"

"It's fine." The squishy warm feeling came back and she slid her fingers through his. "Thanks."

He glanced down at her, and his dimple nearly made her knees give way. "You're welcome." There was a strange note in his voice, something she'd never heard before—as though he hadn't expected her to appreciate his forethought, and the fact she had kind of touched him.

She gave a silent sigh as they went inside. She had it bad. Now she was trying to fool herself that she knew what was going on inside that head of his.

The restaurant had a rustic feel, with semicircular leather sofas around the tables and long mirrors on the walls emblazoned with *Guinness*.

"It's nice here," she said as they took a corner booth.

"Me and my brothers come here sometimes. To get in touch with our Irish roots." He slung her a mocking smile.

"Oh, right." She grinned back. "If I go back far enough I have both Irish *and* Scottish roots. Beat that."

"Won't catch me wearing a skirt."

"You'd look awesome in a kilt. You have the knees for it." To prove her point she gave his knee a squeeze.

He laughed and the tension drained from him. Why had he been so tense? Maybe he'd had a bad day at work. Except he'd been fine when he arrived home. It was only after that phone call that he'd gone all weird.

She wanted to ask him about it, but she didn't want to spoil the mood. So she decided not to tell him about the conversation she'd had with her mom, either.

There was plenty of time for real life to intrude, once she'd made her career plans public.

A couple of hours later, as Paris washed her hands in the restroom, she was smiling to herself again. It happened every time she thought about Cooper, and since that happened a lot, it was a wonder her whole face didn't ache.

He was just so effortlessly considerate. He'd drunk nothing but soda all night, and when she'd called him on it he'd given her a look that melted her panties and told her he didn't need a beer when he had her.

An hour later she was still glowing.

She eyed herself in the black and gilt framed mirror. Tonight she was going to dump this wig, and tomorrow night she was taking him out to the hottest club she could find so she could show him off.

The pub had become crowded since they'd arrived, and she weaved her way through the bodies in the bar. The restaurant was adjacent to the bar, and as she approached the open door she caught sight of Cooper looming over some guy.

She frowned and craned her neck, trying to see what he was doing. Then the other guy turned and slunk off, and she got a good look at his face.

It was the guy who'd chased her and Cooper on the bike.

Hadn't taken him long to track her down. She wasn't going to let it spoil the rest of the night. Another few months and she'd be able to go out anywhere she liked, without being hunted. No one would care if she went shopping in a sloppy tee shirt, or to a bar with a hot, unknown guy.

She couldn't wait.

"All right?" She touched Cooper's shoulder and he swung around. He looked pissed off until he focused on her, and then he let out a long breath.

"Yeah, sure. You want to go?"

That was odd. She nodded in the direction the paparazzo had disappeared to. "Was that the guy we saw the other day?"

Cooper clenched his jaw as though he wished she hadn't noticed that exchange. "He won't be bothering you again."

No, he probably wouldn't. Not once she started college and nobody wanted exclusive undercover shots of her anymore. She took Cooper's hand and squeezed his fingers.

"I'm sorry. I guess I should've worn my cap and shades as well, huh?" She was joking. There was no way she wished she'd worn her usual disguise, but he gave her a strange look, as though he thought she meant it.

But all he said was, "Let's get out of here."

Cooper had already left by the time Paris woke in the morning. She patted his side of the bed. It was stone cold, and she frowned. Why hadn't he woken her up? Come to think of it, they hadn't enjoyed some pre-dawn sex either, and that was a first.

She pushed her hair out of her eyes and sat up. It was only seven. He probably thought he was being considerate by letting her sleep in. So why did she have an uneasy flutter in the pit of her stomach?

The feeling didn't leave even after she'd taken her first caffeine shot of the day. Seriously, she had to get over it. Last week had turned into nothing less than a vacation, but now they were back in Cooper's world, and he couldn't stay in bed half the morning just because she was used to having him there.

It was almost ten before she curled up on the sofa with her cell and clicked to the online tabloids. If there was a photo of her from last night circulating she'd rather know what they were saying about Cooper so she could warn him.

Then she shook her head and took a sip of coffee. He wouldn't care what they said about him. She guessed she just wanted to know for herself.

Sure enough there she was in the black wig, laughing at something Cooper had said to her. He looked gorgeous. She spent a few moments practically drooling over his picture, even though she had the real thing, which she could drool over any time she liked.

She was smiling again in a completely besotted way. Since he wasn't around to catch her, she didn't bother wiping it off her face. Instead, she dragged her gaze from Cooper's sexy as hell photo and caught sight of the heading.

PARIS O'CONNELL'S ROMANTIC TRYST WITH HOT NEW BODYGUARD

Her smile screwed into a frown. How did they know he had been hired as her bodyguard? It pissed her off. She didn't look on him as her bodyguard and never had.

Unable to stop herself she skimmed the first couple of sentences. It was all very generic and blah. Her frown slowly cleared. Maybe the whole bodyguard thing wasn't such a surprise, considering how he had swept her away when they were in the mountains, and how he'd towered over the other guy in the bar. It was a natural leap to make.

Paris looked radiant as she canoodled with her hot new bodyguard in the downtown L.A. bar, Murphy's. *Despite her trademark black wig, there was no disguising the star of* Sunset Heights *who enjoyed feeding her smitten companion from her own plate...*

Ugh. Paris shuddered. She hated to think how Cooper would take being called smitten—and she'd offered him *one* taste of her calamari because he'd never tried it before.

But some bastard had managed to capture the moment on camera.

Scowling she read on. Disbelief spiked through her. What the hell? Disjointed words leaped out at her and she gripped her cell with suddenly sweaty hands.

...since leaving rehab at the age of sixteen...turned her life around...a source close to Paris reveals "no need to keep it a secret any longer".

She'd never told anyone about going to rehab. No one

except Cooper.

He would never betray me like that. She didn't even have to think about it. He had nothing to gain by doing it.

But despite herself, the words danced in front of her eyes. *"…a source close to Paris reveals 'no need to keep it a secret any longer'."*

That didn't necessarily point to the source being Cooper. Even if he didn't think it was something she needed to hide. Even if nobody besides him had ever said that to her before.

Her stomach churned, and she felt sick. She'd trusted him. *I still trust him.*

A persistent little voice in the back of her head reminded her that she'd trusted people before.

They'd all stabbed her in the back. The friends she thought she had when she was a teen, and then Hudson.

She remembered how shifty he had been when she caught him on his cell last night. In fact, he'd acted strangely for the rest of the night. *Who had he been talking to?*

She brutally shoved the thought aside. *Cooper's not like any of them.* He must've said something to the paparazzo in the heat of the moment, that's all. He didn't know what they were like. How they'd twist your words and fill in the gaps.

And then plaster it all over the internet.

She picked up her cell, itching to call him right now and sort it out. But as she stared at his ID she couldn't bring herself to do it. Suppose she was wrong? Suppose he really had sold her out?

She dropped her cell back onto the sofa. She'd wait until she heard from him. She just knew there was a simple explanation for everything.

Chapter Eighteen

Cooper leaned against the door of the gleaming limo and pulled out his cell. He'd picked up his client, Dale, at five that morning from LAX and had spent the last few hours cruising while Dale conducted business meetings in the back. He and Alex had been friends since they were kids, and Cooper had always got on well with him.

It was partly why he'd been so tempted a couple of months ago when Dale had offered him a job on the East Coast. He'd spent all his life in California, and working with Alex was the only legit job he'd ever had.

Not that he'd ever leave *Grayson's*. He'd never leave Alex in the lurch like that.

Ten minutes ago he'd dropped Dale off at the Bel-Air and was now checking his messages. Ella had left a text with a link to an online magazine.

Check this out. E. xo

It took him to a gossip page about Paris. *Fuck*. He'd told that little shit last night to back off. He hoped Paris wasn't too upset she'd been caught with him. It was obvious from the way she'd not thought twice about wearing that damn wig that she wasn't ready to go public.

Because of that, combined with the call from Alex, he hadn't ended up asking her to move in with him. How could he? Right now she was happy staying with him. If he pushed for more she might back the fuck off completely.

He wasn't ready to risk losing whatever they had together.

He skimmed over the piece. Where the hell did they get this shit? And then his gaze snagged on a paragraph under the first photo.

Paris, who's enjoying a short sabbatical before she returns to her hectic filming schedule, is on the shortlist to play Piper Rhodes, the good girl turned bad from Milo Mallory's bestselling novel Payback...

Although, it looks like she can't keep her hands off her gorgeous bodyguards! She's clearly over the ill-fated liaison that had her running back to her old neighborhood.

Paris looked radiant...

He shoved his cell back into his pocket. He knew better than to believe everything he read. They'd even got it wrong about her collapsing on set being the original reason why she left Hollywood so suddenly.

But that bodyguard comment gnawed in the back of his

mind. She had never explained the real reason why she'd turned up at her cabin without even telling her mom where she was.

From the depths of his memory, Scott's voice echoed. *"Can't be any worse than the last jerk she had."*

And then her, giving a delicate shudder as she said, *"He had no sense of boundaries."*

What did she mean by that? Had her last bodyguard come onto her? Had she fallen for him?

A sharp burning sensation speared through his chest— just like it did when she talked about her dipshit ex, Hudson.

Christ. *He was jealous.* It was like a punch to the gut, and for a crazy few seconds he battled the insane urge to smash his fist into the side of the limo.

He'd never cared about that kind of thing before, but the thought of some asshole taking advantage of Paris when he was supposed to be looking out for her made him mad as hell.

Was she in love with her previous bodyguard?

Had she fallen into *his* bed because she was on the rebound?

He wanted her. He'd already faced that, but he sure as hell didn't want to be a substitute in her bed for some other guy.

How the hell am I supposed to ask her about that? He could just show her the article. Wait and see what she said about it.

Except he had to wait another five hours before he could leave work.

Great.

Cooper took a deep breath before he opened his front door. Paris wasn't there to greet him like she had been yesterday. Before he'd taken a couple of steps inside he caught sight of his small dining area.

He stopped dead. The table was set for two, with three tall white candlesticks and shiny cutlery that looked nothing like the odd assortment he usually used for eating. White and lemon flowers with long petals were woven around the candlestick bases and draped off the ends of the table. The square white plates weren't his, either.

"Finally." Paris appeared from the direction of the kitchen. She was wearing a sexy green dress that showed off her gorgeous body, her hair was loose and feet bare. "Any later and all this food would be ruined."

His resolve to ask her about her previous bodyguard wavered. Why spoil the night she'd planned? She'd told him about Hudson and said there'd been no one since. He believed her.

He tossed her a grin and raised his eyebrows. "Food?"

"There's no need to look so surprised. I do know how to find a good caterer."

He laughed and some of the tension that had been eating him up for most of the day eased. "Are you on the menu?" He pulled her close and gave her a kiss. She tasted as good as she looked, and when she dragged her fingers through his hair and sighed into his mouth he shoved the last of his doubts into the corner of his mind.

"Only if you're very good." She pulled back. "Sit down.

I'll bring the asparagus salad over."

He had no idea what an asparagus salad might consist of, but he sure hoped there was more than rabbit food on offer. As she brought over a couple of dishes, he lit the candles.

"I don't recognize any of this stuff." He sat down and watched her flip a thick napkin over her lap.

"That's because I bought all this *stuff* today." She smiled at him, but for some reason that smile put him on edge. There was a bottle of wine in a fancy stand, but he picked up a glass jug filled with slices of citrus and poured them both some water.

He tried not to wolf down the delicately arranged salad, but it was hard, because the portion was tiny and he was starving. Paris, on the other hand, picked at hers as though she wasn't hungry at all.

She whipped his dish away as soon as he finished. His mouth watered for a thick juicy steak. She brought over an oblong plate and placed it before him.

"Lobster."

The artfully arranged lobster with baby vegetables and fragrant sauce looked like it was modeling for a food magazine. "That looks great." He wasn't lying. "Where'd you find this caterer?"

She shrugged. "Around."

He watched her prod her lobster with her fork. Then she took a deep breath and looked up at him. "Cooper."

And he knew. She'd seen that article…and she was upset. He couldn't quite figure out why she'd gone to all this trouble with the meal, but he was taking it as a good sign.

"You probably haven't seen it," she said, which confirmed his suspicions. "But our photos are plastered all over the internet today."

"I did see it." Once again he couldn't help wondering about her previous bodyguard, but she was biting her lip and looked as though she was on the point of running from the room if he said the wrong thing. He reached over and took her hand. "You okay with everyone knowing about us?"

The chances were he'd never have found out if Ella hadn't texted him, but Paris lived in a different world, one that probably revolved around the gossip columns. It burned that she didn't want her Hollywood circle knowing about him. Even if last week she had jokingly invited him to one of those parties. After all, he was hardly in her league.

She frowned and looked confused. "What? Yes, of course." She paused. "Are you?"

Apart from Ella he doubted anyone he knew ever read those kinds of things, but that was hardly the point. "Why the hell would I care?"

She didn't look entirely relieved by his response. "Okay, right. Well, um. This isn't easy…"

Was she ending this thing between them? "What isn't?" His voice was unnaturally harsh.

She let out a long breath. "It's just…nobody but you knows about me going to rehab…and I just wondered… how they found out."

He stared at her. *What the fuck was she talking about?* "How who found out?"

She licked her lips. "You said you saw it, Cooper."

He wracked his brains, but for the life of him couldn't remember reading anything about rehab. Then again he hadn't read it all.

And only then did the implication of what she was really

saying hit him.

"Christ, Paris." In his life he'd been called everything from a *useless piece of shit* to *no good Grayson scum*. From his father to complete strangers who thought they had the right. None of it crushed his chest the way her unspoken accusation did. "You think I told that lowlife?"

"No." Her denial was too fast. "I mean, I don't think you told him on purpose. I don't think you sold me out." She gazed at him with those big green eyes of hers. Did she have the first idea how much her words were killing him?

"Good to know." He couldn't help the thread of bitterness in his voice.

She didn't appear to notice. "But I realized today, you don't know what they're like. They can worm bits of information out of you without you even knowing it. Don't take this the wrong way, but when you speak to them you just have to be...*careful*." She let out another long breath, as though she'd just finished a painful ordeal.

He let go of her hand and flattened his palm on the table between them. "I haven't spoken to the press, Paris. I'd remember if I had."

There was a silence. He could feel his heartbeat in his ears. *She doesn't believe me.*

"But I saw you. At *Murphy's*. When I came back from the rest room."

"Yeah. I caught the bastard trying to sneak out. I told him if I saw him sniffing round you again I'd ram his fucking camera down his throat."

He'd meant it, too. He didn't remember ever feeling so damn mad at anyone before.

She swallowed and avoided looking at him. Instead she

picked up her glass and stared at the sparkling water. "Who were you talking to before we left for *Murphy's*?"

This was just fucking great—and that asparagus must've been off because there was a hard knot in the pit of his stomach.

"It was Alex." His voice was flat.

"Alex? But you looked really weird while you were on the phone to him."

He shrugged and ignored her efforts to try and make him lift his hand so she could hold him properly. "It was just some personal shit."

Another silence loomed between them. Part of him wanted to snatch his hand free from her, but the other half didn't, because he was a fucking fool when it came to Paris.

"Cooper." Her voice was barely above a whisper. He might've ignored her, if not for the waver in her voice.

"What?" He looked up at her, and then he couldn't look away. He knew she was an actor, but no one could fake the tragic expression she had on her face. He battled the urge to pull her into his arms and forget this day had ever happened.

"I'm so sorry." She released his hand and wound her arms around her waist. "I—I have trust issues." Briefly she squeezed her eyes shut. "I always knew deep down you wouldn't betray me, but it's just…I wasn't joking when I said I'm a lousy judge of character. But that doesn't include you."

The knot in his gut eased. "It's okay." It wasn't, but he hated seeing her beat herself up like this. "Forget it."

She took a great shuddering breath. "No. I have to face it. I spoke to my mom yesterday. I might've let something slip to her. I can't remember what I said now, but it's just too much of a coincidence, isn't it?"

He frowned. That didn't make a lot of sense. "Why would your mom do something like that?"

"I don't know. I don't even care." She gazed at him. Tears shimmered in her eyes, and in that moment he knew he was lost. It didn't matter what she said or what she did. He'd do anything to keep her in his life. "The only thing I care about is that I doubted you. I'm so *sorry*..." She sniffled, and a tear trickled down her cheek.

Something deep inside his chest twisted at the sight. He dragged her onto his lap and pushed her hair back from her face. "Paris, stop it. It's over, all right?"

She gave him a watery smile. "It's good that we can talk about things, though, huh? Means we can sort out anything, doesn't it?"

"Sure." He kissed her cheek and could taste her tears. "Let's go to bed and sort out some more stuff."

She cupped his face with both of her hands. "I like the sound of that. Oh wait. We still have the grapefruit sorbet to eat first."

"Screw the sorbet." He stood up and hauled her into his arms. "I've got a better idea."

Chapter Nineteen

"Whoa." Ella rounded on him as soon as he entered the office. It'd been three days since the scene with Paris, and tomorrow she was going back to Hollywood for a magazine promo shoot. She hadn't mentioned college again.

"Did you *know* what was going to happen?" Ella said. "Twitter's gone crazy with it!"

He'd grown up with Ella, but sometimes he had no idea what she was going on about. "What?"

She gave a dramatic sigh. "The murder, of course. I don't suppose even Paris knows who did it, does she? They'll drag it out for the next year."

"Drag what out?"

She narrowed her eyes at him. "*Sunset Heights*. Lola was brutally murdered in last night's episode. Talk about a grand exit. Paris never breathed a *word* about it the other night at your gran's. I guess this leaves her well and truly free to follow a movie career now."

Paris hadn't told him, either. Why would she keep that secret, when she'd told him about her college plans? She hadn't even told him *Sunset Heights* was on last night.

"Guess so." Wasn't much else he could say.

Ella cupped her chin in her hand. "How's married life treating you then?"

It was the second time over the last couple of days she'd said something like that. She seemed to find it hilarious that he was living with a girl, when up until Paris he'd never even dated anyone.

"Not what I expected." Wasn't that the truth—but living with Paris, even this strange temporary kind of living together, wasn't what kept him awake at night.

It was the thought of making it permanent. But he still hadn't even asked her to move in with him properly. He had no idea where this relationship was heading. So why he kept thinking of doing something as fuck awful scary as Jackson was planning with Scarlett was beyond him.

Except, the thought of not having Paris in his life, scared him a damn sight worse.

"Wow. She's really got you by the balls, hasn't she?" Ella grinned. "Never thought I'd see the day. You and Jackson under the thumb within a month of each other."

"Hardly."

"So what's going to happen when she goes into movies? You thinking of moving to Beverly Hills with her?"

"Shut it, Ella. I'm not moving to Beverly Hills."

"So what's Paris up to today? Reading scripts or something?"

"No." He frowned. "Kind of strange. Her mom arranged

for her to have a spa day." She'd said it was her mom's way of apologizing. Neither of them had said it out loud, but he guessed they were both thinking it was an apology for spilling the shit about her rehab.

Strangely, Ella hadn't once mentioned that to him, and he knew she'd read the article. Then again, she read a lot of celebrity gossip so maybe she knew half of it was garbage in any case.

The door buzzed, and Ella raised her eyebrows. "Not expecting anyone." She checked the intercom video feed and frowned. "Some woman. Hang on." She picked up the handset. "Can I help you?"

Ella cocked her head and looked up at him. "One moment." She muted the intercom. "You'll never guess. It's Cora O'Connell, and she wants a word with you. You here or in Mexico?"

What the fuck? There wasn't much that made him nervous, but the thought of Paris's mom *having a word with him* came close.

He let out a long breath. Mexico was preferable, but knowing Cora O'Connell, she wouldn't give up until she'd seen him. He might as well get it over with.

He gave Ella the nod, and she screwed up her face in sympathy before activating the lock. The door opened and Paris's mom entered, looking like she'd just stepped off a catwalk.

She swept her gaze around the office. "Hi, Ella," she said, as if they'd seen each other just the other day instead of ten years ago. Then she turned to him. "Cooper." Her smile didn't reach her eyes. "It's so good of you to see me. Is there somewhere we can talk?"

"Sure." *Shit*. Should he have greeted her first? Too late to worry about that now. He waved her through to his office, and as she passed by him he caught Ella's eye. She crossed her fingers, which didn't exactly boost his confidence.

He shut his office door behind them. Cora sat and eyed him. Should he sit behind his desk? Or on the edge of it? In the end he opted for behind his desk. The more distance he had from her the better.

"Paris doesn't know I'm here," she said. "I'd prefer to keep it that way."

He just bet she did. He steeled himself for a barrage of abuse.

"May I count on your discretion?"

He felt like a ten-year-old kid again on the receiving end of Cora O'Connell's dignified disapproval. "She won't hear anything from me."

"Thank you." Cora crossed her ankles and leaned very slightly toward him. "The information I'm about to share is privileged."

"Okay." He had no idea what else she expected him to say to that.

"Did she tell you…" Cora hesitated for a second. "Why she left home so suddenly?"

Because she wanted to sort out her future. He was sure Cora was leading him into a trap but couldn't figure out how.

"She just wanted some time out."

Cora's smile didn't budge. "Did she mention her previous bodyguard at all?"

He hoped his expression was as unreadable as Cora's. "Only that he was a jerk."

"Ah." Cora gave a brief nod. "So she didn't say anything

about the unfortunate… incident involving him?"

Although it looks like she can't keep her hands off her gorgeous bodyguards!

The words ground through his mind like a rusty saw. He never had asked her about that. She'd been so upset that night, he hadn't wanted to make things worse—and afterwards the moment had passed.

"It's not important." He knew there was a low note of warning in his voice, even though he tried to contain it. Not that it seemed to bother Cora.

"You're right of course," Cora said, which caused his unease to magnify about a million times. There was no way he could see her agreeing with anything he might say. "It was just a silly fling but I'm afraid Paris took it rather badly. I just wanted her to have a little break to clear her head. I didn't think she'd go quite this far with things."

She's clearly over the ill-fated liaison that had her running back to her old neighborhood.

Something hard lodged in his chest. Why hadn't she told him the truth about her last bodyguard? Or was Cora just messing with him?

"As far as I know she made the decision to leave Hollywood herself."

Cora waved her hand in a gesture that reminded him of Paris. "She did. But…" Cora paused and he couldn't help feeling it was completely calculated. "You may not be aware that she's been offered the role in a major movie." Even he could hear the pride leaking out of every word. It took him a couple of seconds to actually process what she'd just told him.

No, he hadn't known that. All Paris had said was she'd

had a couple of callbacks. Come to think of it, they hadn't talked about this movie role at all. He'd just assumed she wasn't going for it, since she was heading to college.

He didn't want Cora knowing that. So he gave a non-committal kind of nod.

"Has she told you anything about the part?"

It'd be a great part to land. He remembered her saying that at his gran's, but that was about the most she'd ever talked about it. "Not really." He felt admitting that was going to cost him.

Cora's smile appeared to warm, as though his answer was a relief. "Well, once I told her the role was hers she was ecstatic, as you can imagine. But you know what Paris is like. Such a perfectionist. I tried to talk her out of it, but she does have a very stubborn streak."

What the fuck was she talking about? No way was he going to ask her, so he simply stared her out. After a few seconds she appeared to realize he wasn't going to take the bait, and she gave a little sigh.

"She wanted to live the part for a few days. The movie's about a famous pop star who falls for a guy from the wrong side of town. She just wanted to get into the headspace for a while."

"Is that right?" For a creepy moment he sounded like Alex. "And you expect me to believe that?"

Rich girl slummed it so she could be with her bad boy hero. He hadn't taken a lot of notice while she had been talking about the movie at his gran's. That didn't mean he hadn't heard what she was saying.

He'd thought she was such a great actor. *But when had she been acting?* With his family at the tea—or with him?

"No," Cora said. "I don't expect you to believe that. Whatever you might think, I don't dislike you, Cooper. I never have."

She might be Paris's mom, but that could only take her so far. He leaned into her space, his eyes never leaving hers. "What's this really about, Cora?"

For the first time she appeared genuinely uneasy. Then she took a deep breath and the mask was back on. "If she doesn't take this role, her career's over. No one's going to touch her again if she's flaky and unreliable. And here's the thing. She's wavering because of you, Cooper. You've gone from being her muse to her potential nemesis."

His chest ached. It reminded him of the time his father had put him into the hospital with broken ribs, only this pain was worse.

"She wants to go to college." His words sounded hollow. Cora's gentle smile was a knife through his heart.

"Whenever there's a crisis she says she wants to give it all up and go to college. She never goes through with it. Do you know how many times she's deferred taking up places?"

How the hell would he know something like that?

His silence gave Cora all the answer she needed. "Acting is her life. This movie is the big break she's been hoping for. Do you think she should throw it all away…for you?"

"I'd never ask her to give up anything."

"I know." For a second he saw a flicker of emotion in Cora's eyes, but maybe he just imagined it. "But she will. She has it in her head this is what she wants, and in a few months' time, when she's climbing the walls because she's not doing the one thing she loves more than anything else in the world—it'll be too late. She'll be blacklisted."

Paris hadn't been using him. He wouldn't believe it.

You sure about that? She could have anyone she wanted. She'd chosen him.

But why had she? He was no great catch. He was a fucking liability. Paris was out of his league. He'd always known it. But he'd hoped…

"There wasn't anything you could do about what happened to Alex." Cora's voice was soft. Gentle. *Understanding.* "But there is something you can do for Paris. Walk away, Cooper. Give her the chance to make something of her life."

She couldn't be any clearer. *You screwed up Alex's life. Don't do the same to Paris.*

Cora stood up. "Don't be too hard on her. This might've started out as a game for her, but the trouble with Paris is —" Cora sighed and dropped her gaze to the desk. "She always falls for Lola's love interests on *Sunset Heights.* It's what she does. I'm used to picking up the pieces. She soon gets over it."

Cooper's head pounded. *She hadn't lived the last week as though she was on some fucking soap.* Just because he'd found the dinner elaborate and kind of strange didn't mean she'd only done it for show. *She comes from a different world…*

Cora walked to the door, then she paused and looked over at him. "I know you'll do the right thing. I know you care about her. And…" She bit her lip and for a split second she again reminded him of Paris. "I'm sorry."

He sat there, staring at the door after she closed it behind her. He'd promised Cora he wouldn't tell Paris about this meeting, and he wouldn't.

He wouldn't act on it, either. If Cora thought he'd give

up the best thing that'd ever happened to him, she was fucking insane.

She's mine. She was a shining star in his life. At odd moments during the day he'd catch a hint of her perfume clinging to his clothes. Or he'd remember something she'd said, and a warm glow rolled through him. Fucking corny, but it wasn't like he was going to shout it from the rooftops.

In her arms, for the first time in his life, he felt *needed*. As if he wasn't a complete waste of space and good for nothing but fucking up people's lives. She made everything...right.

He didn't know how long he sat there, but finally he went online and did something he'd been meaning to for the last week.

He watched her infamous *Sunset Heights* Christmas episode.

Chapter Twenty

It was late afternoon before Paris arrived back at Cooper's apartment after her spa day. Which had been great. All that gardening last week had pulled muscles she didn't even know she had. *Would've been a lot more fun, though, if Cooper had been there.*

She'd have to suggest that to him. She could just imagine the look on his face if she told him they were getting an ultimate couples package. In fact, she'd just go ahead and book it for their month anniversary. How cool would that be?

She still hadn't taken him out anywhere. That was going to change once she got back after her photo shoot, but first she was going to have to confront her mom.

Her happy mood faded. Her mom had called a few times in the last three days, and she had ignored her, except to send one text confirming she'd be back for the shoot tomorrow. It looked like her message had finally been received, since the next text had been the day spa olive branch.

She pushed her mom out of her head and made her way to the bedroom to pack some of her things. Cooper was giving her a ride back to the cabin first thing in the morning so she could pick up Scott's car. Her brother had called her the night before, completely pissed that she hadn't arranged for its return yet.

Weird. He hadn't said anything about her and Cooper being together. Was it possible her mom hadn't told him?

Then again, she hadn't either, and the opportunity had been perfect. But was it really fair, when she hadn't run it by Cooper first? He might want to tell Scott himself.

Why hasn't he told Scott about us already?

It was almost seven by the time Cooper got home. He hadn't answered the couple of texts she'd sent him, but her annoyance at being ignored melted the second she caught sight of him.

"And you've brought dinner." Looked like Chinese. God, she hoped she fit into the clothes for her photo shoot. Though, if she had put on a pound or two—or even if she hadn't—they'd still Photoshop her until she was their ideal of perfection.

Whatever.

Cooper dropped the takeout bags onto the kitchen counter and pulled her into his arms. She draped her arms around his neck and smiled up at him. His dimple was nowhere in sight, but it didn't matter.

He didn't need to smile for her to know how much he wanted her.

His kiss was raw and hungry, like he hadn't seen her in a week. She scraped her nails across the back of his neck and he gripped her ass, hauling her tight against him.

She came up for air. "Dinner's going to get cold, you know that?" *Like I care.*

"I've got a microwave." He popped open the buttons on her shirt and pushed it over her shoulders. Before she could toss it across the kitchen he hoisted her onto the counter.

"I take it back. Dinner's going to be *hot* tonight." She leered at him, but he didn't laugh at her. He didn't even smile, which was weird. Her comment was definitely worth a flash of his dimple.

"You're always hot." He made it sound like that wasn't such a good thing. Unease shivered through her.

"Is everything okay?" She pushed her fingers through his hair, forcing his head back so he had to look her in the face instead of her boobs.

"Yeah." He finally gave a crooked smile, and her insides melted. "You're gorgeous, Paris. I can't get enough of you."

That was more like it. She arched her back and hooked her feet around his butt. "You can have me anytime you like. Over the sofa, in the kitchen…" She gave him a wicked grin. "I've never done it on stairs, either. Just for future reference."

"We've got all night." His voice was rough and he shoved her short skirt up to her ass. "I'll fuck you in every room if that's what you want."

Whoa. She wriggled on the hard kitchen counter. "Sounds good to me." Her voice was hoarse. He stroked her thighs, and with every upward caress his thumbs nudged her sensitive folds. "Hope you've got a condom in your pocket."

He leaned in. "Don't worry about that. I've got plenty

for tonight." He kissed a hot trail along her jaw to beneath her ear, and then down her throat. She closed her eyes, tilting her head back so he had complete access.

I can't get enough of you, either. He sucked her nipple through her bra and cupped her breasts, as though he wanted to eat her alive.

Another shudder rocked through her. Prickles raced over her skin. Not just where he touched, but *everywhere,* as though he'd lit a flame inside and she was burning up with need.

He pulled her to the edge of the kitchen counter, and she clung onto his biceps as he ripped open his jeans. *God, I love his arms.* Her gaze dropped, and she watched, fascinated, as he sheathed himself. She loved his cock, too.

I love every gorgeous inch of him. Inside and out.

He hooked her panties aside. The air was cool against her wet flesh but only for a second as Cooper grasped his cock and teased her sensitive clit.

"Aim and fire," she croaked, but instead of shooting her a grin, he looked as though her sick humor was a knife through his chest. "Cooper," she whispered. "What's wrong—?"

His mouth silenced her with a savage kiss, and he thrust into her.

This was all she needed. She dug her nails into him. He filled her so completely. He grasped her ass before she slid across the counter and pounded into her as though this was their very first time.

It always felt like the first time with him.

She pushed her tongue into his mouth, giving him everything...and he took it, nipping and sucking and driving her out of her mind.

The sound and scent of sex filled her senses. His mouth on her skin. His hands on her body. She never wanted this moment to end, but she couldn't hold on any longer.

With a choked gasp she arched into him as her orgasm hammered through her. He came at the same moment, gripping her butt so hard, pain and pleasure collided.

God. Her head dropped to his shoulder as she sucked in air. Her heart thundered, and aftershocks throbbed between her thighs. He held her as though the world was ending—and if it was, there wasn't any better way to go.

Cooper stared down at Paris. Her hair was tangled across the pillows and there was a soft smile on her face.

She was beautiful. He sucked in a jagged breath that hurt his heart.

He'd watched those *Sunset Heights* episodes. No wonder she'd won an award. She made the cheesy lines she'd had to say sound deep and meaningful, and even though he had no idea of the storyline, her scenes had still grabbed him by the throat and not let go.

She deserved all the critical acclaim she'd received. After watching the episodes he'd trawled through the press about her. They all agreed she was wasted on the soap.

Cora had been right. She hadn't intended to leave Hollywood for college. She was leaving her soap for movies.

All he'd been was a distraction that got out of hand. They had never had a hope. She belonged among the stars, and he had never moved far from the gutter.

He lifted one of her curls, and her hair slid between his

finger and thumb. *I don't want to let you go.* But he'd never really had her. Whether he'd caught her on the rebound or not wasn't even the point anymore.

If he did nothing, she would stay with him. She'd ruin her chances of making it big. It didn't matter that he'd give up everything and anything to make her happy. How could it work between them when he was the one holding her back?

His eyes stung. *You're fucking crazy.* How could he even think of letting her go when she was the reason this last week had been the best time of his life?

How? Because he'd screwed up Alex's life, and he wouldn't do the same to Paris.

He trailed the end of her curl across his face and breathed in her gorgeous scent. It was the last time he ever would.

*C*ooper *is acting so weird this morning.*

Paris eyed him as he brought her luggage down the stairs, but the grim expression on his face didn't budge.

"It's only for a few days," she reminded him, as he dumped the small overnight case she'd bought the other day by the front door. "I'll be back before you know it."

He gave a noncommittal grunt but didn't return her smile. She bit her lip as he stomped off toward the kitchen. She'd been avoiding the issue but she couldn't any longer.

Was he pissed by her assumption that she'd move back in with him before she went off to college? They'd never discussed it. She'd just assumed it was okay. Well, if it wasn't, why hadn't he said anything?

She cleared her throat and followed him into the kitchen.

Now was a shitty time for a heart to heart but maybe that would at least clear the air. "Hey. I've been thinking. If it's too cramped here with me, I can always stay in a local hotel when I come back."

She held her breath. *Tell me not to be so fucking stupid. Tell me you don't ever want me to move out.* Sure she wouldn't be living with him 24-7, but the East Coast wasn't the end of the earth. They'd still see each other plenty of time.

Slowly he turned to face her. Her heart jackknifed, although she wasn't sure why. But she was sure something was wrong. *God, no…*

"It's been fun, Paris. But it's time to move on."

Move on? What the hell did that mean?

You know what it means.

No. He wasn't breaking up with her. She didn't care that they'd never made it official. They'd dated.

What about last night? How could he want to end things after last night?

"You don't mean that." Where was her famous acting ability when she needed it most? She sounded exactly the way she felt. *Disbelieving. Shell shocked.*

This was his idea of a joke. She was going to fucking kill him because it wasn't funny…

"We both know it was nothing serious. Thing is, I won't be here even if you do come back."

Her stomach pitched. *I'm going to be sick.* Nothing serious? He really believed that? Even after she'd told him things she'd never told anyone else?

She wanted to wrap her arms around herself, curl into a ball, and weep. Instead she grabbed Lola with both hands and hid behind the girl whose face was plastered across every tabloid in the country.

"Oh?" Her voice sounded brittle. Nothing like Lola. She dug deeper. "Where are you off to then?" Yeah, that would do. He'd never guess her stupid heart was breaking into a million tiny pieces. *Bastard.*

But there was no force behind it. He wasn't a bastard. He was Cooper Grayson, and she loved him.

He shrugged, as though it didn't matter. "Haven't decided yet."

Right. That told her. The pain in her chest wrapped around her heart. She was going to die. But she wasn't going to die right here in front of him.

"So, is this something you've just decided on, or what?"

"Nah. Been thinking about it for a while."

You never told me. Why did that hurt so much?

God, I'm so stupid. She'd thought their time together had meant as much to him as it did to her. He might not sell her out to the press, but he sure as hell had managed to crush her hope she'd finally found someone who could love her just for herself.

He'd never mentioned love. All he'd done was treat her like a regular girl. And when she'd thrown herself at him he'd done what any other red-blooded guy would've done.

It didn't mean he loved her.

She swung away from him before he saw the truth in her eyes. *No wonder he never told Scott.* Because he'd never intended anything permanent.

Neither did I. Not at the start. When had it all changed from an exciting fling into an even more exciting promise of something more?

Doesn't matter. It had all been in her head.

"I've called a cab," he said, as though he had no idea her world was crumbling round her ears. He *didn't* have any idea, that's why. "Thought that'd be better than me giving you a ride. Scott can pick his own car up from your cabin."

Her throat was clogged with unshed tears, but she hadn't won the Viewers Choice for nothing. "Good idea." She couldn't face him, though. Right on cue, as though this was an episode from her soap, the door intercom buzzed, announcing the arrival of her cab.

Cooper walked her down to the street, held the cab door open for her, and gave the driver a wad of notes. "See you," he said. The sun was in his eyes and she couldn't see his expression, but she wasn't sure she wanted to.

"Sure." She sounded like she didn't give a rat's ass whether she saw him again. "Bye."

He didn't even hesitate. He slammed the car door and then stood there, arms folded, watching until they turned the corner and she couldn't see him anymore.

Chapter Twenty-One

The following afternoon Cooper steeled his nerves and pushed open the door to *Grayson's*. Once a month Alex held an informal meeting so they were all aware of how things stood with regard to the firm. Yesterday he hadn't been near the office, and just as well. After watching Paris disappear, the last thing he'd wanted to do was face his brothers with their inevitable questions about what the fuck he thought he was doing with Paris O'Connell.

He wasn't doing anything with her anymore.

All day her face had haunted him. The look of shock when he'd lied through his teeth to her. The tears she hadn't been able to hide fast enough in those gorgeous green eyes.

She was a great actor but deep inside he didn't—*couldn't*—believe she'd used him.

You wish.

And every time he thought that he came back to the big question.

Why would Paris O'Connell want any kind of future with him?

But suppose he was wrong? Suppose she really had been serious about going to college, and putting her career on hold had nothing to do with him at all?

It doesn't matter. She was better off without him — and it was about time he finally faced Alex and told him he wanted to take up Dale's offer to work for him.

"Hey, Ella," he said as he entered the office. "Alex here yet?"

"Yes, sure. He's in his office. J should be here in a minute so we can get started. I don't want things running late. It's my evening at the sanctuary."

Ella spent half her life at her animal sanctuary. Before he had the chance to catch Alex alone in his office, Jackson arrived and the meeting began.

It was hard to concentrate when he knew how badly he was going to let Alex down, but he couldn't remain in L.A. Even though the chances of seeing Paris again were zero, the thought of staying in his apartment twisted his gut.

She'd only been there a few days, but everywhere he looked he saw her. And he wasn't just talking about the bits of furniture and things she'd bought.

His apartment smelled of orange blossoms. That was hard enough. It would be a damn sight worse when the last lingering hint of her scent finally vanished.

Alex was talking about expanding. Guilt coiled through him. How could he leave now, when work was picking up?

You're taking an awful lot of credit for the ways things've turned out. Paris's voice echoed through his mind. He shifted on his chair and folded his arms.

Hell I am.

He took no credit for the way Alex had turned his life around.

Alex made his own choices.

And it was past time he made his.

"Coop." Alex leaned across his desk. He was frowning. "You okay?"

Cooper took a deep breath. "I'm fine." *Now or never.* "I'm thinking of taking up Dale's offer."

The silence was deafening.

"Dale Mathers?" Jackson said just as the silence got awkward. "You serious? He wanted you to move to the East Coast."

"I could do with a change of scene." Sweat trickled along the back of his neck. Alex was just staring at him with that mask, the one he'd never had before he'd been sent to juvie.

"This got anything to do with Paris?" Ella frowned at him, but it wasn't a pissed frown...more curious.

"No." He let out a breath and finally looked Alex in the eye. "This is about me. I need to get away. I'm thinking of going to night school."

He'd told Paris he wished he'd gone to college. Until now, he hadn't known just how much he did want that. He'd barely finished regular school, and he'd rarely bothered turning up to classes.

He wanted more now. Much more. And while he'd rip out his own tongue before admitting it, the truth was, working for Alex was suffocating him.

"Okay." Alex leaned back in his chair. Cooper couldn't tell what he was thinking. "If that's what you want. There'll always be a place here for you when you want to come back."

Take it.

He couldn't. "I don't know if I'll be back."

"It'll be good for you," Ella said. Then she turned to Alex, who looked like he'd turned to stone. "You've been saying you wanted to put out feelers. See how things are in other states. We're expanding here, but look ahead. Why can't *Grayson's* expand nationally?"

"There's a thought," Jackson said.

Alex still didn't say anything.

A n hour later the meeting finished. Cooper had a few more scheduled jobs but after that he'd be off.

A strange combination of relief and freedom rolled through him. The guilt was still there, but it didn't grip his guts the way it once had. After his initial silence Alex seemed okay with his decision. Maybe one day he'd come back to *Grayson's*. If he did, it'd be because that was his choice, and not because it was the only option open to him.

They all left the office together. Ella was trying to get Alex to go with her to her sanctuary. Again. She never gave up.

"I'm not into small furry animals." Alex looked as though Ella had asked him to shovel shit or something. "I donate. What more do you want from me?"

"What the fuck." Cooper froze. On the other side of the street was the guy who'd taken photos of Paris in *Murphy's* — and he was making his way toward them.

Alex pushed Ella behind him. Without a word, Cooper's brothers flanked him, both positioned slightly in front of him. A shudder inched along his spine.

All his life his brothers had protected him as best they could. Even now, when they had no idea what the problem was, their first thought was to shield him from danger.

He broke ranks and stepped forward. "What're you doing here?"

The guy stopped about six feet away. "You've got fans," he said. "Want to give a quote on how it feels to be loved and discarded by the darling of Hollywood?"

"I'll give you a quote," Jackson said. "You can take your camera and shove it up your fucking ass."

Cooper raised his hand, and Jackson shut up. Of the three of them, Cooper had always let his mouth run away with him. There was plenty he'd like to say to this guy, but there was no point.

It'd get twisted. It'd get back to Paris. She might hate him right now for how he'd treated her, but he didn't want her to despise him.

"No comment."

The guy gave a half smile. "Must be hard, having your childhood sweetheart choose to go back to her mom rather than stay with you. But hell, Cora O'Connell has balls of steel."

Childhood sweetheart? Was that the way the story was being played? At least Paris knew the score. She'd know he hadn't made that shit up.

Wouldn't she?

"I've been following Paris for a couple of years now," the guy said. What the fuck was the matter with him. Did he have a death wish? "For what it's worth, I've never seen her looking the way she did that night I caught the pair of you in *Murphy's*. Like she was really happy. Guess that's something, huh?"

"I've got nothing to say to you." He turned and marched toward the parking lot. With every step the paparazzo's words rang in his ears.

Must be hard, having your childhood sweetheart choose to go back to her mom rather than stay with you.

Except she hadn't made that choice. He was the one who'd broken up with her. Paris hadn't gone back to her mom. She'd gone back to Hollywood because she had a photo shoot scheduled.

He hadn't given her any choice at all.

"Shit." He gripped the handlebar of his bike and fought the urge to double over. *What had he done?*

All his life his brothers had looked out for him. From the age of twelve he'd been Jackson's right hand man on the streets. They'd never discussed it. They were brothers. And when Alex set up *Grayson's* there was no question that he and J would join.

They were brothers. Guilt had driven him to skip school so he could watch Jackson's back, and guilt over Alex going to juvie was why he'd stayed at *Grayson's* even when he realized he wanted more from life.

He'd pushed Paris away because he was afraid guilt would kill him if she stayed.

But he hadn't fucking asked her what she wanted.

Jackson slapped him on the shoulder. "You want to talk about it?"

"No."

"Sucks, right?"

Cooper glared at his brother. Jackson had a grin on his

face, as though he found this situation funny. "Fuck off."

"Take your own advice, bro." Jackson still looked amused, the bastard. "Seems to me you're in love with Paris O'Connell."

Talk about throwing good advice back in your face. He'd said that to Jackson about Scarlett barely two weeks ago. Ella would call it karma that he now found himself in the same god-awful mess.

Do I love her? He'd never even thought about it before. Just knew having her around was so right. And now that she was gone, nothing made sense.

"I've screwed up."

"It's what the Graysons do." Jackson gave him another slap on the back. *Do that again…*

"I told her it was just some fun. I don't think she'll ever speak to me again."

"You can't have screwed up worse than I did with Scarlett. We managed to work it out."

His brother didn't have a clue.

Neither did he.

Chapter Twenty-Two

Paris's new bodyguard hustled her to the waiting car. The photo shoot had dragged on all day, not helped by the fact everyone wanted to talk about Lola's shock demise three nights ago.

She closed her eyes as the car sped off and ignored her mom and assistant's excited conversation on how fabulously the day had gone, and oh, by the way, which restaurant were they going to now?

"I don't care," she said without opening her eyes. She guessed she was being a little mean to her mom. After all, she'd been really understanding since Paris had turned up yesterday, red-eyed and spoiling for a fight. Instead of giving her twenty questions she'd just given her a big hug.

It was a relief not having to tell her mom Cooper had dumped her from a great height. She wasn't sure she could've stood seeing the *I-told-you-so* look on her face.

Her agent Marcia was already at the restaurant when

they arrived. Not that she cared, but why had her mom even asked for her opinion if they'd already decided on this one?

The three other women discussed the impact of Lola's dramatic exit until she wanted to scream. Instead, she checked her Facebook account on her cell. Cooper hadn't left any message. Not that she'd expected him to.

Whatever.

"Honey." Her mom leaned across the table and tapped the screen of her cell. "Did you hear what Marcia's been saying? She's been approached by three different producers today regarding high profile movie projects."

Paris took a deep breath. She'd had well over a week to come up with a calm and well-reasoned speech on what she planned to do, but figuring out how she was going to tell her mom about her future was the last thing she'd focused on when Cooper was around.

He sure as hell wasn't around any more. She'd felt horrible when Hudson had ditched her, but that was nothing compared to how hard it'd been to crawl out of bed this morning—like a lead weight was crushing her heart. Luckily the photographer today had wanted a moody pout. She wasn't sure her acting ability could've coped otherwise.

There was no easy way to say it. "I'm going to Brown."

Her mom didn't even miss a beat. "Paris, honey, it's great they still want you, but we have to strike while the iron's hot. And you've never been hotter than right now."

"Hmm," Marcia said. "You know we can work around college if you want to."

Her mom waved her hand. "Paris has to be *here*. It's no good her being on the other side of the country, is it?"

Her chest tightened and it was hard to breathe. It was a

familiar sensation but that didn't make it any easier to cope with. "Mom, we talked about this last year." *When you persuaded me to defer for a year.*

"I know." Her mom smiled at her. "Look, I'll have someone call them and explain. I'm sure they'll be happy to defer your place for another year or two."

She didn't want someone to call them. She didn't want to defer for a year or two. Why the hell couldn't she just tell her mom what she wanted?

"I want to start this fall."

"Paris, you have the world at your feet right now. You can do anything you want. If you disappear for three years you might as well kiss your career good-bye. No one will remember you, let alone want you."

Cooper had thought it was a great idea. He hadn't said she was crazy for wanting to put her career on hold. *Oh God, she missed him.*

She stood up. "I'm going to Brown." Before she lost her nerve again, she turned and walked out of the restaurant. So she wouldn't have to look at anyone while the car was brought round, she dragged out her cell and went online.

An image of Cooper by his bike, head bowed, with Jackson by his side, leaped out at her.

Paris Does a Lola & Leaves Sexy Cooper Heartbroken

Hot bodyguard Cooper Grayson was unceremoniously dumped by his childhood sweetheart, Paris O'Connell...

Fighting back emotion, macho Cooper faces the world alone once again...

"Paris, we need to talk about this." Her mom appeared by her side and there was the faintest note of panic in her voice. Then she caught sight of what she was reading.

"Honey, it's for the best. It was never going to work."

I could've made it work.

"Whatever." Somehow she couldn't stop staring at his photo. He looked…crushed. Or was that all in her mind?

"Childhood sweetheart?" Her mom leaned in closer. "Well, I guess that's nice of him, saying you were the one who ended things."

She frowned. She hadn't told her mom which of them had ended it, although she supposed it wasn't hard to guess. "Mm."

Her mom took a breath. "He didn't want to stand in your way. He knows you're going places. He'd only hold you back."

Her stomach heaved. She sure as hell hadn't told her mom any of *that*. "What makes you so sure he was the one who broke up with me?"

"What? Well, you've been so *sad*…"

"He didn't want to stand in my way?" Her hands were sweaty and her legs were shaking. Her mom blinked at her, as though she had no idea what Paris was going on about.

"Well, I'm assuming…I mean that would be the reason why he…Paris, what's this all about?"

What's this all about? She gripped her cell and hitched in a shallow breath. It didn't help the tightness crushing her chest.

"That's not why he broke up with me."

"Okay. Then the best thing you can do is go all out for this Milo Mallory movie. That'll show him what he gave up."

"My God, you don't miss any chance do you?" *Where the hell had that come from?* But now her mouth wouldn't stop. "*You* were the one who told him to dump me, weren't you?

Because you wanted me back here where you can control every fucking thing I do."

"Paris." Her mom's shocked whisper didn't make her feel bad the way it usually did. Because *her own mother had fucked up her life.* "How can you even say that? Everything I do is for you, honey."

Paris knew people were looking their way. She ignored them. *Take as many damn photos as you want.* For the last couple of years she'd gone along with everything her mom wanted, hoping things would change—but nothing would change if she didn't make her stand.

"Is that why you leaked the fact I'd been in rehab to the press last week?"

Her mom sucked in a sharp breath. "I would *never*—"

"I know it wasn't Cooper." It hurt, knowing her mom would stoop so low, just to get her own way. "Is that why you went to see him, because I didn't blame him for that gossip and run back home?"

If it had been anyone but him, her mom's plan would've worked. But Cooper wasn't like that. She had trusted him.

I still trust him.

"I don't want you to throw your life away on someone like Cooper Grayson."

Fury burned through her chest, and all the little resentments that she'd buried over the years finally came bubbling up.

Yes, Mom loves me. No, it doesn't mean she can rule my life. It was past time her mom faced that, too.

"Don't talk about him like that. He's the best thing that's ever happened to me."

"What?" Her mom stared at her as though she'd lost her

mind. "But he's nobody, honey. He can't help your career or—"

"Stop right there." She leaned into her mom's space. "Why would I want him to help my career? He doesn't give a *fuck* about who I know. Do you have any idea how good that feels?"

Her mom opened and shut her mouth, but for once nothing came out.

Just as well. She wasn't in the mood to take any more of her mom's crap. "From now on, you stay out of my personal life. It's none of your business who I date."

"*Paris.*" Her mom's voice was all choked up, as though she'd been horribly wronged.

It was a good thing the car arrived right then. Paris glared at her mom, got in the car, and slammed the door. Then she called her brother.

"Scott? I need a huge favor."

When it counted, her brother wasn't a dick at all. He ditched his plans so he could go with her to the cabin. It had nothing to do with him picking his car up from there, because why would anyone do that at ten at night?

"You want to tell me what's going on?" Scott said as she drove her car toward the mountains.

She didn't answer right away. She might be mad as hell with her mom, but that didn't stop the ache deep inside, or the guilt that she'd confronted her in public. She hoped nothing had been recorded.

"I told her about Brown. She's not happy."

Scott grunted. "She was never going to be happy about it. At least it's done now."

"There's something else." Had he really not seen any of the gossip about her and Cooper? "She warned Cooper to stay away from me." God, that pissed her off so much. Tension knotted her shoulders, and her guilt for swearing at her mom vanished.

"Cooper?" She could hear the frown in his voice. "Don't tell me she believed all that shit in the gossip columns. That's insane."

She let out a puff of breath. "It wasn't shit."

There was a long silence. "Are you telling me…?" His voice trailed away. Obviously he was having trouble processing the thought.

"Yeah. I'm in love with him. Deal with it."

Two hours later they were almost at the cabin before Scott had come around to *dealing with it*.

"So, I need this favor," she said, when his threats of bodily harm against Cooper had slid into the less volatile *he better not fucking hurt you* territory.

"I'm doing you a favor now. What the hell do you call this?"

"This isn't the favor. This was just to get you alone."

Scott muttered a few obscenities under his breath. She ignored him.

"I need you to ask Cooper if he'll meet me at the cabin some time this week. Just to talk things through. Will you do that for me?"

"I'm not a dating agency."

When she glared at him, he scowled back. "Fine. I'll ask him. Not promising I won't break his nose, though."

She snorted. "You wish." She turned down the dirt track that led to her cabin. As it came into view she frowned when the headlights picked out a Harley parked out front.

God. Was that…?

"Looks like I won't have to be your messenger." Scott made to get out of the car and she grabbed his arm.

"No. Promise me you won't do anything. I need to speak to him, Scott." Maybe he had dropped by simply to pick up the things he'd left behind last week. She hoped it was more than that. Maybe he'd wanted to leave her a note or something.

Scott didn't look convinced. "I'll give you ten minutes. Don't make me want to bleach my eyes when I come in."

Huh. She'd love for Scott to have to do that, but she wasn't at all sure things would go that well.

At the door she hesitated. Suppose her mom's interference hadn't been the reason why Cooper had ended things? Suppose he really had meant what he said and she was about to make herself look like the biggest idiot in the history of the universe?

There was only one way to find out.

Chapter Twenty-Three

Cooper finished checking the water pressure in the shower and stepped back. He'd been working on the plumbing for hours so Paris wouldn't be having cold showers anymore.

It wasn't much of an apology, but until he worked out how he could get her alone so he could grovel—Jackson reckoned groveling was the only way he stood a chance—the flowers and chocolate and fuck knows what else would have to wait.

He frowned. That thump sounded like the front door. He grabbed a wrench from his toolkit and inched open the bathroom door. If a burglar was out there, he was about five seconds away from needing a trip to the ER.

Paris blinked at him. He nearly dropped the damn wench on his foot.

"Hi." She sounded wary. "Didn't expect to find you here."

It suddenly occurred to him he had no right being here

at all. Just because he still had a key from last week didn't mean that she couldn't accuse him of breaking and entering.

"Uh." What the fuck was that? When had he ever been at a loss for words?

She looked at the wrench and appeared to find it fascinating. "So… How are you doing?"

He cleared his throat. "I just stopped by to fix your plumbing."

That got her attention. "My *plumbing*?" She sounded as though she didn't know the meaning of the word. "You've fixed the shower?"

"I said I would." He shifted uneasily. This wasn't the conversation he'd planned on having with her when he saw her again. For a start, he didn't have any flowers and chocolate and fuck knows what. "Photo shoot go well?" He managed not to cringe, but only just.

It didn't help when she just stared at him as though she didn't have a clue what he was talking about. He gripped the wrench tighter and tried to ignore the sinking sensation in the pit of his stomach.

She was a vision. In a sexy little dress and matching jacket, she looked like she'd stepped straight off the red carpet.

Whereas he was covered in grime and sweat.

"It went fine."

The silence was agonizing. Was it possible to grovel when all you had to offer was a fixed shower?

"Congratulations on landing the movie role." That'd show her he knew all about her change of plans without them having to discuss it. *Does this count as groveling?* He didn't think so.

She frowned at him.

"I haven't landed any movie role."

Cora had lied to him.

He could hardly accuse her mom of lying. He transferred the wrench to his other hand and kept his mouth shut.

She took a deep breath. "Did my mom tell you that?"

He couldn't answer her without letting on that Cora had paid him a visit. He made a noncommittal grunt and shoved the damn wrench into his jeans' back pocket.

"And you believed her?"

How was he supposed to answer that? "Look, it doesn't matter to me if you make multimillion dollar movies or give it all up and go to college. Whatever makes you happy. I'd never stand in your way."

She bit her lip. For a terrible second he thought he'd made her cry. "I know you wouldn't." There was a suspicious wobble in her voice. He took her hand and squeezed her fingers, and she didn't pull back.

Tell her. He swallowed. Here came the grovel. "I didn't mean what I said—about it just being some fun. Although it was fun," he added hastily in case she jumped to wrong conclusions. "But it was much more than that."

"Mm." She took a step toward him. The scent of orange blossoms drifted around him, and he breathed in deep. God, that was good. Like he'd come home. "Do you still want to move on?" she asked.

He tugged her a little closer. "Only if you're there with me."

She gave a funny little smile. "That could be arranged."

Their foreheads touched. This was all he wanted. He didn't need to know anything else, but his big mouth opened and out came the words. "Why did you really run away here last week?"

He steeled himself for her answer. Whatever it might be. She didn't pull away, or glare at him, or try and laugh it off. Instead, she shuddered and her fingers tightened around his.

"Oh God, it was awful."

He'd asked. Served him right if he didn't like the answer. "What was?"

She shook her head. "You can't breathe a word about it."

"You really think I would?"

"No." She sighed. "I know you wouldn't. But it's just… Okay, I know I'll get over it and blah blah whatever, but it's seriously gross walking in and seeing your own mother doing it doggy style with your bodyguard."

What the…

"Your mother?" he asked, in case he'd just had a crazy hallucination.

"Yes." She scrunched up her face. "Doesn't bear thinking about it, does it?" She opened her eyes and stared at him. "Please don't ever think about it, Cooper."

"That's the reason you left Hollywood and left a false trail to Europe? Because you caught your *mom* having sex with your *bodyguard*?"

"*Please* don't keep saying that."

Cora had deliberately made it sound as though Paris had somehow been involved with her bodyguard, without actually lying about it. She should be in movies herself.

The knot in his chest loosened. She hadn't been on the rebound. Not even close.

You still haven't asked her what she wants. It shouldn't be so hard, but despite everything he was afraid of her answer.

"What do you want to do, Paris?"

She tensed. "What do *you* want to do?"

They could fuck about like this all night. He knew what he wanted. "I want us to be together. We can make it work. Just say the word."

She cupped his jaw in that way she had. It was tender and sexy all at the same time. Then she moved in close, as though she didn't care that he was covered in dirt from crawling about on the floor.

"Yes," she whispered. "I want that, too. You and me against the world."

He wanted to fork his fingers through her hair and drag her into his arms, but his hands were filthy. He pulled on the end of one of her curls instead. "Not against the world, babe. Whatever you decide, I'll always have your back."

"Cooper Grayson." He'd never get tired of hearing her say his name like that. "That's the third nicest thing anyone's ever said to me—and you get first and second place, too."

He laughed and tugged her into his arms. To hell with her clothes. "Paris O'Connell, I don't know why you want to be with me, but I'm not ever letting you go."

She wound her arms around his neck and threaded her fingers through his hair. "I'm going to hold you to that. For*ever*."

Forever. He'd never thought about having a *forever* with anyone before. No one before her had wanted him for anything serious. He was good for a laugh, nothing more. He was the one who'd ruined his brother's life.

Except he hadn't ruined Alex's life. Paris was right. People made their own choices. There was a choice he could make right now—to let the moment go, or tell her how he felt.

There were no roses or violins or a big romantic moon by the ocean. Just the two of them in a run down cabin that needed a whole lot of TLC.

He took a deep breath. *Now or never.*

"I love you, Paris."

She smiled up at him. "It's about time." Her voice was all husky, and hell, were there tears in those gorgeous green eyes of hers? "I'd almost given up on you."

"Don't ever give up on me, babe."

Her sigh wrapped around his heart. "I won't. I love you, Cooper. I always will."

He kissed her.

You're my heart...

"Fuck me." Scott's disgusted voice stabbed through the moment, and he and Paris turned to look at him. He didn't let go of her, though. She kept stroking the back of his neck as though she didn't give a damn her brother was watching them.

"Hey, Scott," he said. He guessed it was too late to warn his friend he was seeing his sister.

"Eye bleach," Scott muttered, glaring at Paris. She smiled sweetly.

"If you're staying the night you can use Cooper's old room. He's with me now."

A strange ache throbbed through his chest. This was what he'd wanted. For her to publicly acknowledge they were together. It was never the wig that was the problem. It was his conviction that, deep down, she was ashamed of being seen with him.

He kissed the top of her head, then caught Scott's gaze.

"Guess checking out the talent at *Thirteen* isn't going to happen now?" It was a challenge. It was also a no-brainer.

"Not in this lifetime," he said, before he scooped Paris into his arms and carried her into their bedroom.

Epilogue

"This is a lovely wedding," Paris said, as they danced in the small ballroom of the hotel where his brother and Scarlett had tied the knot earlier that day. "Pretty romantic having it in the same place Jackson proposed, huh?"

"Guess so."

She frowned. "Are you okay? You've been kind of distracted all day."

"I'm fine."

No, he wasn't. He was having serious second thoughts about the birthday surprise he'd arranged for her in a couple of weeks' time.

He knew she'd receive some outrageous gifts, and the fact was she could afford to buy anything she wanted, but he'd discovered by chance she'd never been to Paris. Not that she ever said she wanted to, but it seemed like fate.

He wanted to do something for her that she'd never done before.

It'd seemed a great idea a month ago when he'd booked them for a long weekend in a small hotel hidden down a secret alley. He'd planned it all out. They'd see all the famous sights, and then on the final evening he'd arranged for a private cruise along the river Seine. While she admired the glittering lights of the most romantic city in the world, he was going to ask her to marry him.

The closer the date got, the worse he felt. Suppose she said no?

"Hey lovebirds, having a good time?" Ella wrapped her arms around his and Paris's shoulders. "Scarlett knows how to put on a good show doesn't she?"

"I was just saying to Cooper how romantic it all was."

Ella pulled a face. "Coop wouldn't know romance if it smacked him in the face."

"Thanks, Ella."

"You're welcome." She flashed him a smile. He'd shared part of his plan with her, just to make sure he was on the right track, and she'd been seriously impressed. He hadn't told her about asking Paris to marry him. Though he had a sinking feeling Ella might've guessed.

"So have you decided whether you're going for that movie part?" Ella asked.

Paris turned and leaned her back against him, and he linked his arms around her waist. "Yes, I am. Marcia's just smoothing out some kinks in schedules for next year, but it should work out fine."

When she had taken her place at Brown, she'd decided against going for the roles her mom had so desperately wanted for her. But after talking to her agent, she'd come to another decision—one where she could pick and choose her own movie roles, and still get the degree she'd always wanted.

"Guess your mom's happy about that."

"She's coming round to it. In fact, I think she's kind of enjoying having more time to herself now she's not shadowing me. She and Anson seem to be getting quite, uh, serious."

He hid his grin. When they were alone she might shudder about the fact she'd caught sight of Anson's naked ass, but at least he was keeping Cora occupied. Which could only be a good thing, since Paris had acquired a new manager.

"Paris, I want to ask you a favor." Ella gave a bright smile, and with a shrug Paris untangled herself from his arms.

"Sure."

Cooper watched them disappear in the crowd. What the hell was that all about? Ella wasn't going to spill his secret, was she? As far as Paris was aware they were going to hang out at the cabin for her birthday weekend, just the two of them.

Alex appeared by his side. "How's the East Coast treating you?"

Of course Ella wouldn't say anything. He dragged his attention to his brother.

"Good. Dale's keeping me busy."

"No regrets?"

He knew Alex wasn't just referring to the move across the country.

"No. She's all I need."

There was a long silence. "Okay," his brother said at last. "Keep in touch."

Cooper gave him a sideways glance. Of course he'd keep in touch. Even though they'd both relocated to the East Coast three months ago, they were always flying back. A couple of months ago he'd gone with her to some huge *Sunset Heights* party, and last month she'd shot a new ad for the perfume contract she was still under. He always caught up with his brothers and gran while he was here.

And once she finished college they'd most likely move back to L.A. With the business degrees he was working on, he'd have a lot more to offer *Grayson's* in the future.

He headed toward where Paris and Ella had disappeared and caught sight of Ella's rainbow hued hair. She was alone.

"Damn, you've got it bad, Coop." Ella shook her head. "Take that look off your face. I haven't scared her off. She's out on the terrace, that's all."

"What did you say to her?"

"Nothing." Ella shrugged. "Well, nothing to do with you. She still thinks you're putting together a surprise party at the cabin for her birthday."

"Okay." Then he swung around and kissed Ella's cheek. "Alex is over by the bar if you want him."

Ella gave a brittle smile. "What makes you think I want him? I've got a hot football player waiting for me on the dance floor."

Right. He frowned as he watched Ella stalk off, then he shook his head and made his way to the terrace. Paris was by the door, watching him.

"What was that all about?" He took her hand.

"Oh, she just wanted to know if she could stay at the cabin for a few days next week. Not sure why she wanted to get me alone to ask that, but whatever."

Neither did he. "You want to get some air?"

"Sure." She leaned her head against his shoulder as they went outside. Wall lanterns cast a glow, and they strolled further along the terrace, away from the other guests who'd stepped out to enjoy the mild fall night.

She sighed softly and wrapped her arm around him. "This is perfect."

Yes, it was. He rubbed his jaw across the top of her head and inhaled her gorgeous scent. The full moon was huge in the night sky, and its reflection rippled on the surface of the lake. An abundance of roses were twined around the wrought iron railings that surrounded the terrace.

From inside the hotel came the faint, haunting sounds of violins.

A shiver inched along his arms. They weren't by the ocean but everything else was…

Perfect.

"Are you cold?" She frowned up at him. "Want me to warm you up?"

There was no one else in this corner of the terrace. No one who'd see if he fucked it up—or if she rejected him.

He gripped her hand. If she said no, he wasn't going to let her run away. "I'm taking you to Paris for your birthday."

Hell. That wasn't what he'd meant to say. She gasped and looked thrilled.

"*Are* you? Oh my God. That's awesome."

He grabbed her other hand for added courage. "It was going to be a surprise."

"It *is* a surprise. It's the best surprise ever." She squeezed his fingers. "I've always wanted to go to Paris."

He glanced at the moon for inspiration. The only thing

that filled him was cold terror.

How the fuck had Jackson asked Scarlett? He should've asked his brother for some advice.

There was no easy way to say it. "Will you marry me?"

Her smile seemed to freeze. *Shit.* Now what? As if to mock him, the violins reached some kind of crescendo.

"You want to marry me?" There was a wobble in her voice. *Is that good or bad?*

"You're the best thing that's ever happened to me." *Christ.* Was that the best he could come up with? Even if it was the truth.

"Am I?" Now she sounded as though she was about to cry.

He should've waited. Stuck to his plan. Although how this would be any easier in France he had no idea. "We can wait. I don't want to rush you into anything, but you need to know. You're all I want. You're all I'll ever want."

She blinked a few times, as though she had something in her eyes. "You always say the best things, Cooper."

His heart hurt. It could've been worse. She could've told him *no way.* "Hey, maybe I'll ask you again in a year or so."

She went rigid. "What d'you mean you'll ask me again next year? You're not wriggling out of it that easily, Cooper Grayson. As far as I'm concerned you're my fiancé as of right *now.*"

He stared at her. "Did you just accept my proposal?" It sure hadn't sounded like it.

"Well of course I did. Are you crazy?"

Was he? "You want to be my wife?" *Damn that sounded good.*

"Only as much as you want to be my husband." Then she

laughed and fell against him. "I love you, Cooper Grayson. Don't you ever forget it."

Like that would ever happen. She'd changed his life. "Love you, too, Paris Annabelle Sofia O'Connell." All he wanted to do was get her alone and show her *exactly* how much he wanted to be her husband. "How soon can we get out of here?"

The End

Acknowledgments

I want to give a big shout out to my fabulous Street Team for all the friendship and support you've given over the last year. You guys are the best! Thanks also to Sara Hantz and Amanda Ashby for the brainstorming and cyber chocolate. Huge thank you to my amazing editor, Candy Havens, for making me dig so deep. Big cheers to Ellie and Debbie and everyone at Entangled Publishing for making it all so painless! And thank you to Mark, for everything.

About the Author

Christina Phillips is an ex-pat Brit who now lives in sunny Western Australia with her high school sweetheart and their family. She enjoys writing paranormal, historical and contemporary romance but whether the hero is a fallen angel, tough warrior or sexy mortal, the romance will be sizzling and the heroine will bring her hero to his knees. She loves hearing from her readers!

Christina is addicted to good coffee, expensive chocolate and bad boy heroes. She is also owned by three gorgeous cats who are convinced the universe revolves around their needs. They are not wrong.

www.christinaphillips.com

Discover the **Grayson Brothers** *series...*

Hold Me Until Midnight

Scarlett Ashford needs a date for her father's wedding. Only she doesn't just need a guy in a suit—she needs a bodyguard. Except that Jackson Grayson is big and gorgeous and way too sexy. So much so that Scarlett's tempted to let this hot bad boy ruin her oh-so-good reputation. Besides, one hot and incredibly intense night between a bad boy and a pampered princess could never turn into something real...could it?